TROUBLE
Don't Last Always

Sherry Jones

TROUBLE DON'T LAST ALWAYS

Copyright © 2017 Sherry Jones
All rights reserved.
ISBN: 1548967076
ISBN-13: 978-1548967079

This novel is a work of fiction. Any references to real people and entertainment entities are intended only to give the novel a sense of reality and authenticity. Any resemblance or similarity to other names, characters, locations and events is coincidental.

No part of this book may be reproduced or stored in any form or by any means, mechanical or electronic, without written permission from the author except for brief excerpts for book reviews.

Scripture quotations are from the New King James Version of the Holy Bible. www.biblegateway.com

Copy Editor: Nichole Gause
www.moreabundantlifesite.com

Cover design: Britny Logan
www.linkedin.com/in/britnylogan

Author's Photo: Regina Brewer-Shannon
www.gigiuniquedesigns.com

*In loving memory of my parents, Rufus and Elouise
Ford, whose love and guidance
helped shape me into the woman I am today.
You are forever in my heart.*

ACKNOWLEDGEMENTS

First and foremost, I would like to thank my Lord and Savior, Jesus Christ. Without you, I would be nothing. I am thankful for the gifts you have given me, and I pray you are glorified through this work.

Extra special thanks to my loving husband, Willie, for your never-ending support through this journey. You believed in me even when it looked like I was spinning in circles and things wouldn't come to pass. You are my rock, my love, my heart and I'm so blessed to share this life with you.

To my son, Devin, thank you for being Mommy's biggest cheerleader. Knowing you are proud of me and looking up to me keeps me going. Thank you for inspiring me to be the best I can be for you.

To my bonus daughters, Crystal and Raven, thank you for supporting my dream. We are not connected by blood, but by love and I'm so thankful for that.

Thank you to my content editor, Nichole Gause, for your guidance throughout this project. You were a godsend and helped me shape my vision into the work of art it has become.

Thank you to my cover designer, Britny Logan, for your beautiful work. You are truly gifted, and I appreciate you sharing your gift on this project.

Last, but not least, I would like to thank all my family, friends, church family and Toastmasters family for your support. Many of you have listened to me talk about this dream for years. Thank you so much for your encouraging words when I needed it most. Thank you for reading early drafts, pushing me to keep going and loving me through it all. The time has finally come, and I couldn't have done it without you.

Chapter 1

My eyes burned as hot tears rolled down my face. The pillow beside me was empty, but the scent of too much cologne still lingered in the air. The jeans, T-shirt and sneakers on the floor were gone and I was alone. I closed my eyes, trying to wish it all away, but I could still feel his presence.

I could still feel his gentle hands cupping my face, see his gorgeous green eyes locking with mine and smell his spearmint scented breath as he leaned in for a kiss. We gave in to our desires and although I knew God was not pleased, my body thanked me. How could something be so right and so wrong at the same time? My emotions were spinning like a hurricane. I grabbed the phone and called my best friend, Georgia.

"What's wrong?" she exclaimed when she answered

the phone.

"I slept with Roger!" I yelled through my tears.

"Oh, that's all."

"What do you mean, that's all? This is big!"

"I thought someone was hurt or dead. It's two o'clock in the morning. Anyway, I knew it was going to happen eventually. I'm not surprised," she said as she let out a huge yawn.

"How did you know? If you saw something, why didn't you warn me?"

"You don't need me to warn you. You're a grown woman. I figured you wanted it to happen."

"Why would you say that? Of course, I didn't want this to happen. I've been celibate for over four years..."

"Maybe it's been four years too long. You've been playing with fire for months. He's your baby daddy. I get it."

"What?"

"Maybe you've been celibate because you know that's what a single Christian woman is supposed to be, not because that's what you really believe in."

"Why are you talking to me like this? I'm calling you for comfort and you're questioning my spiritual walk. I'm not perfect and neither are you!"

"I'm just calling it like I see it. I wouldn't be your

friend if I didn't keep it real."

"I don't need real right now."

"Well, that's what you're going to get. You know I don't sugar coat things. You need to put your big girl panties on and deal with it," she snapped.

"Bye Georgia!" I yelled and slammed down the phone.

I was a twenty-seven-year-old woman, not a child. How dare she talk to me like that! She acted like she never did anything wrong in her life, but she did all kinds of scandalous things before she met her husband. Who was she to judge me?

I paced back and forth. I wasn't angry with Georgia. I was angry with myself. How could I let my guard down with Roger? Why didn't I resist temptation? I loved him so much even though I knew he didn't love me the same.

I ran to the bathroom to take a shower. Maybe the filth of what I did would go down the drain with the water.

The hot water burned my skin, but I didn't care. I closed my eyes and pretended the water was cleansing my insides as well. It was flowing through my mind, my heart, my soul and taking away everything that was not like Christ. It was purifying me. I began to pray.

Dear Lord, please forgive me. My body wanted the touch of a man, any man. No, not just any man. I wanted Roger. I wanted what we once had. I wanted to feel his touch, lay in his arms and melt into his kiss. I love him so much. But, I know none of that makes it right. None of that repairs my broken promise to you. Lord, help me! Lord, restore me! I want to start over. I need to start over. Please hear my cry. In Jesus' name. Amen.

My body shivered when it hit the cold air and I quickly put on my robe, wiped away the steam and stared into the mirror; searching for something resembling
myself.

Roger always said I had the most beautiful dark brown eyes he had ever seen. He loved my slender nose, full lips and gap-toothed smile, but all I saw was guilt, shame and confusion. I knew I was forgiven, but I didn't feel redeemed.

I changed my sheets and after much tossing and turning, drifted back to sleep. I was awakened by the phone ringing.

"Hello," I said sleepily.

"When are you coming to get this boy?" asked my

sister Monica.

"What?" I asked, trying to wake up.

"Look, Maureen. You need to come and get him now. I told you I had a meeting this morning. You don't care about anyone else's time, but yours."

"I'm sorry I'm running late Monica. I will be there in a few. It's not that big of a deal."

"That's your problem Maureen. You don't take anything serious. If I was the one that was late you would make a federal case out of it. But I guess common decency doesn't apply to you, huh?"

"What's your problem? I'm on my way. We will finish this conversation later."

"Whatever," she said and hung up the phone.

Monica was always doing something to make me want to spit fire. She had been a thorn in my side ever since our mother died. At that moment, I was expected to become a mother figure to someone who was only two years younger than me. It wasn't fair to either of us. I was only twelve and didn't know much about anything. She just wanted her mom, not an imposter. Our dad became a referee, spending way more time stopping us from fighting than parenting. We loved each other. There was no doubt about that, but friction was our constant friend. If I said the sky was blue, she would say it was orange, just to spite me.

I threw on a red and black sundress and my favorite black sandals, jumped into my beat down Honda Civic and sped to Monica's house. My thoughts were bouncing around like jumping beans and I had no idea how I got there. Once I arrived, I could refocus on my agenda; to put Monica in her place.

Monica lived in a beautiful two-story home with sunshine yellow siding and white shutters. I always admired its wonderful curb appeal, but that day I wanted to kick over the plants and flowers that lined her driveway.

Monica came bolting out of the door as I was getting out of the car. Her slender frame was dressed in a beautifully tailored navy business suit and pumps. Her hair was pinned up in a perfect bun and her makeup was flawless as always.

Moments later, Josiah ran out behind her. His eyes were as big as silver dollars and filled with tears. He ran into my arms and held on tightly. She threw his bag onto the ground, twisted her perfect lips and put her hands on her hips.

"Go home Maureen! You don't ever have to come back to my house again!" she yelled.

"What's wrong with Josiah? Why is he so upset?

What did you do to him?" I asked firing questions like assault missiles.

"I ain't done nothing to that boy. He's upset because I said you were a selfish person who thinks the world revolves around her. I swear you get on my last nerves!"

"I get on your nerves? You and your nasty attitude get on mine. You're the one who thinks it's all about Monica. It's what Monica wants or else. You need Jesus!"

"Don't give me that Jesus stuff, Maureen. I have a relationship with Jesus and I'm fine just the way I am. I don't need to act like you and those folks in your church. Y'all aren't nothing but a bunch of hypocrites anyway!"

When she said hypocrites, thoughts of what happened the night before flashed into my mind. But I repented, so I'm okay, I rationalized.

"I know He didn't tell you to act the way you are right now. Don't you ever throw Josiah's things again! You're scaring him."

"He's going to experience things way scarier than me throwing his bag."

"What do you mean by that?"

"Look at him. When the world looks at him they see a White boy; white skin, green eyes. That's why people don't think you're his mama. I bet there's no problem when he goes out with that no-good Daddy of his. But, when he's out with you, people think you're his babysitter."

Josiah hugged me tighter and whispered "Mommy, let's go" but I was too involved in the verbal sparring with Monica to notice.

"People are ignorant. His complexion may be white, but anyone with eyes can see that he has my features.
I can't believe you would bring that up. You've never talked like this before."

"Well, some things can't be swept under the rug anymore. Let's lay ALL the cards out on the table!"
Her nosy neighbors were beginning to come out of their houses. I didn't want them to enjoy the spectacle we were making out of ourselves. Monica, of course, didn't care. She just got louder.

"You come over here with your high and mighty 'I'm a better Christian than you' attitude and you don't think it bothers me. We got saved at the same time before the same altar or don't you remember that?"

"Yes, I do. It was at Daddy's funeral. The minister said Daddy was smiling down because his girls had come to Jesus," I said softly.

"So how can you question my salvation?"

"Being saved is more than accepting Jesus as your Savior and being baptized. You must make Him Lord of your life. You have to live your life according to His Word."

"Humph! So, you do that all the time? I don't think so. What's done in the dark will come to light, Maureen," she snarled and looked me up and down.

I prayed my evening with Roger would never come to light. That was one secret I wanted to die with.

"We all make mistakes, Monica. We aren't perfect, but we must pick ourselves up and keep trying. It's like you stopped trying."

"Amen, sister!" said Ms. Annie Parker from across the street.

"Look everyone. The show is over. Maureen is leaving. Right, Maureen," Monica said forcefully.

"Yes, I'm leaving. Let's go, Josiah. Say goodbye to Aunt Monica."

"Bye, Aunt Monica," he said to my stomach.

She didn't hear him because she was already in the house, slamming the door behind her.

Chapter 2

Georgia and I decided to go out to eat after church the following Sunday. Josiah was spending time with Roger, so I had some free time. It had been over a week since Roger and I had sex and neither one of us brought it up. I just wanted to forget about it.

We decided to eat at Crossroads Inn; the birthplace of the town's founder, John T. Cross, converted into a bed and breakfast. On Sundays, they served a delicious buffet meal and invited local jazz and gospel groups to perform. It was always overflowing with all types of people. There were the "after church" folks, the "lazy Sunday, don't want to cook" folks and the "tourist" folks.

Georgia was treating this time. She said it was to apologize for being short with me the other night, but I know she just wanted to be a blessing. She was such a good friend. I couldn't believe all the negative things I had thought about her.

Georgia was beautiful inside and out. She was what the fellas called thick. At a size 14, she was big enough to be called plus size, but she wouldn't be considered fat.

Her almond shaped eyes danced as she talked about some of the behind the scenes drama with the singers in the church choir. The choir always ministered beautifully and knew how to usher the Holy Spirit into the midst of the people, but there were always some ungodly goings on before they came out. Georgia was a member of the choir and always shared the scoop with me.

"Girl, Pat Bishop was so upset because Darryl cancelled her solo at the last minute. She asked him why and he said the Holy Spirit told him the atmosphere needed a different song. You know he is very sensitive to the Spirit."

"What did she say?" I asked with anticipation.

"She told him he needed to clean the wax out of his ears because he obviously didn't hear the Spirit clearly. Can you believe she said that?"

The laughter spilled out of my mouth, loud and hearty. I knew people were looking, but I didn't care. Georgia was giggling also.

"That's crazy! So that's why she was sitting in the congregation today?" I asked.

"Exactly! He sat her down really quick."

"I don't see how you deal with those people in the choir, girl. They are hilarious."

"Well, I won't have to deal with them much longer," she said.

"What do you mean?" I asked with caution. I knew it wasn't good news because her body language changed. She hung her head down and her beautiful crown of natural curls fell into her face. When she looked up I saw tears in her eyes.

"Martin and I are leaving Faith Chapel," she said barely above a whisper.

"Why?"

I couldn't believe it. I met Georgia when I first joined Faith Chapel. She was the teacher of the adult Sunday school class. I was so thirsty for the Word back then and she provided me with the knowledge that quenched it. We started having conversations after class and the teacher/student relationship developed into a true friendship. Faith Chapel wouldn't be the same without her.

"Martin and Pastor Green have a difference of opinion and he says we can no longer sit under him."

Georgia's husband, Martin was serious about his Christian walk. He knew the Word and was bold about his convictions. He was studying to become an ordained minister. I knew if he had problems with Pastor Green they were big. Once Martin made up his mind about something there was no changing it.

"What kind of difference of opinion, Georgia?" I asked, afraid of the answer.

"It was about his ordination."

"What about it?"

"Pastor Green doesn't feel he's ready even though he's completed all the classes and the board has approved him. Martin has been under Pastor Green's discipleship for three years now and I think he's just ready to complete everything. Pastor Green has expressed his concerns to the board, but he really can't stop him. Martin talked to Pastor Johnson at Grace and Deliverance and they will have his ordination there and accept him as their Assistant Pastor."

My mouth dropped. I couldn't believe what I was hearing. Martin was going to defy Pastor Green's concerns, go to another ministry and take my best friend with him!

"I hate to say it, but I agree with Pastor Green," she said under her breath, but loud enough for me to hear.

"Why, Georgia? If anyone is ready to be ordained I would think it would be Martin. He has been faithful and studied so hard. You told me how he would be up until three am studying and then go to work at seven. That's commitment."

"It takes more than commitment, Maureen. Martin lacks some things spiritually. I've been praying, but the Lord just hasn't given me peace about it. When I talked to Martin about it, we got into a huge argument."

"You told Martin you didn't think he was ready? I know he went off."

"Yes, he did. He was so angry. His face turned red and he yelled repeatedly. He told me I wasn't a supportive wife and reminded me I was supposed to submit to him. He started quoting Ephesians 5 and I zoned him out. I couldn't take it, so I walked away and went into our bedroom. He got even more upset and he's sleeping in the study every night since. I don't know what to do, Maureen!"

She put her face into her hands and burst into tears. I didn't know what to do either. All I could do was to whisper a prayer.

Lord, please give her peace. Heal the hurt she's feeling. Let her feel your loving arms around her. Help her to feel your love. You created marriage to be holy, so we know you will bless it. Bless her marriage right now. Right now! In Jesus' name. Amen.

I got up, gave her a quick hug and kiss on the cheek and sat back down. It took her a little while longer to calm down, so I just continued to whisper my prayer until she lifted her head.

"Thank you. I needed that. I know our friendship is divinely ordered. You always know what to do," she said, wiping away the tears and blowing her nose with a napkin.

"You're welcome sweetheart. You know I love you and I will always be here for you."

"Let's talk about something else. I'm finished with heavy conversation. I'm going to go back up and get some more chicken," she said as she got up from the table.

Oh my God! I can't believe this is happening. I must do something about it. Maybe Martin doesn't understand how this is affecting her. I'm going to talk to him and straighten this out.

My thoughts were interrupted by my cell phone ringing. I looked at the caller ID and it was Roger.

"Yes," I said, irritated.

"Hey Maureen. When will you be home? I need to drop Josiah off. I'm going to watch the game."

"And why can't he watch the game with you?" I

asked, rolling my eyes.

"Because I'm not watching it at home."

"Where are you going, Roger?"

"Look, I don't have to tell you nothing. You just need to tell me when you will be home."

"When I get there," I said and hung up the phone. I knew he wanted to go to Man Man's house and smoke weed. Roger thought he was so cool because all his friends were Black. All he wanted to do was hang out with them and smoke. He didn't know they talked so much junk when he and I got together. They just tolerated him because when they wanted to get high he would provide the weed. I thought about telling him, but it would have been a waste of time, energy and my precious breath.

"What's wrong?" Georgia asked as she sat back down.

"We may need to cut this short. Roger is acting crazy. He's ready to get rid of Josiah."

"Oh," she said and wrinkled her face.

"I know what you're thinking."

"No, you don't."

"You think I shouldn't care what Roger wants. He doesn't spend enough time with Josiah anyway. You think I should stop dealing with him, especially after the other night. You think...."

"Please stop telling me what I think. Since you know so much, you don't need for me to tell you anything. We'll just leave it at that."

That was Georgia's way of ending the conversation and it worked. We didn't say another word to each other until we finished eating and went outside to our cars. We said our goodbyes and promised to call each other later that night. It was a promise we would both break.

I decided not to go home, but rather go to Roger's house and pick up Josiah myself.

Roger lived with his mother. He said it was so he could help her, but I knew it was the other way around. Roger had a hard time keeping employment because he was always causing trouble and being disrespectful to his employers. He once told his boss he was going to set his own schedule because he needed to have a life. His boss told him he surely could set his own schedule, at home.

They lived in a small white wood framed house. Their grass always needed cutting, although Roger was there and didn't have anything else to do. They shared an older model Honda Accord, but Roger could have had his own car. There was an old Chevy Impala in the yard that he was supposed to fix, but didn't.

His mother liked garden gnomes, but she didn't have a garden. The little statues filled their front yard and porch in random places. She also loved wind chimes and had at least a dozen hanging from their porch. On a windy day, it sounded like an orchestra gone mad.

When I pulled up I was more than shocked by what I saw. There were three police cars parked in front of the house. Roger's mother was on the porch trying to hold her robe closed around her robust body while pleading with the police not to take her son. Her brown hair was all over her head and her hazel eyes were filled with tears. Roger and his friends, Man Man and Tick, were in handcuffs being led to the cars. I scanned the scene frantically for Josiah, but he was nowhere to be found. I ran up to Roger, bypassing two police officers.

"Where's Josiah?" I screamed. Roger's handsome face was filled with pain and a longing for any moment other than the one he was experiencing.

"Who are you, ma'am?" the police officer asked wearily like he had enough drama for the day.

"This is my baby's daddy and I need to know where my baby is!"

"You need to calm down, ma'am."

"Where's Josiah?" I asked Roger again, ignoring the police officer.

"He's in the house, Maureen,"

I ran towards the door, nearly knocking Mrs.

Michaels down. Once inside I ran from room to room screaming Josiah's name.

I didn't hear a response until I opened the door to the bathroom.

"What's wrong, Mommy?" Josiah asked. He was taking a bath oblivious to what was going on outside.

"Why are you taking a bath by yourself?"

"I got dirty when I went outside to play so Daddy put me in here."

Oh, my God! Roger was so irresponsible. How could he leave Josiah in the tub with the door closed? My heart was pounding out of my chest. I tried to breathe slowly so I would calm down.

"That's great, honey. Let's finish up so we can go home."

"I'm not ready to go. Daddy and I are going to watch TV."

"You have to do that another time. We must go now."

"No, Mommy! I don't want to go!" he screamed at the top of his lungs and started kicking his feet, splashing water everywhere. I didn't have time for one of his tantrums.

"We are going, Josiah, and that's it! Let's go!" I said, lifting him out of the tub.

After I got Josiah together, I could take inventory of

the chaos around me. The house looked like a hurricane hit it. Papers and books were everywhere. Plates of old food sat in the living room. The kitchen floor was beyond dirty, and dishes were piled up in the sink. The bedrooms were horrible too with all kinds of junk stacked up on the beds. I had never seen the house like this. Mrs. Michaels always did her best to keep things tidy despite Roger's messy behavior. Since her husband passed away three years prior she seemed to care less and less about appearances. I guess the desire for cleanliness died with him.

Mrs. Michaels was sitting on the couch in the living room with a blank stare on her face. She didn't like me, and I didn't like her, but I needed to know what happened.

"Are you alright? What happened?" I asked.

"You people is what happened! His no-good friends got him in trouble, then here you come raising cane and grabbing up that boy. The only reason why I let y'all come around here is because of Roger. If I had my way, I wouldn't have anything to do with any of you," she said, getting up and pointing her finger in my face.

I wanted to slap her finger out of my face and curse her out, but the Jesus in me stopped me in my tracks. She better be glad the old Maureen wasn't standing before her. If so, it wouldn't have been pretty.

"Mrs. Michaels, if Roger got in trouble, it's his own fault, not his friends or mine. What did they get him for this time?"

"Possession of crack cocaine. They were going to sell it, I think," she said, lowering her finger and looking down.

"I wouldn't be surprised if he's been using too. I thought he was trying to change. He told me he was going straight. I should have known better," I said, shaking my head.

"I don't know how much his bail will be, but I figure the two of us could come up with it."

"The two of us? You mean the one of you! I'm not putting up the money to get Roger out of jail and I'm not helping you. You think you can talk about me and my son and I'm going to help you. You must be crazy!" I screamed.

"I'm sorry, Maureen. I'm just angry and desperate. You know he is my only child and now that his father is gone, he's all I got."

"Well, I'm sorry, but I can't help you. I barely have money to take care of Josiah and me. I don't have any to waste, helping someone who doesn't want to help themselves. Tell your grandma goodbye, Josiah."

"Bye, Grandma," Josiah said, giving her a hug. She hugged him tightly and for a long time.

She was so full of contradictions. She was saying such hateful words, but I could tell that she loved Josiah. She may not like the fact that he was Black, but he was still a part of Roger and that fact alone granted him all the love her heart could give.

"Let's go, Josiah," I said, pulling him away from her.

"Bye," she said and burst into tears.

When I walked outside, the police cars were gone, but there were still people hanging around. I saw a few of them look at me and laugh. I didn't care if I never came back to that house again. I wanted to get as far away as possible as quickly as possible.

"Why doesn't Grandma like you, Mommy?" Josiah asked as I strapped him into his booster seat.

"What makes you think Grandma doesn't like me?" I asked, wondering where this conversation was going.

"I heard her call you a mean name. Daddy got mad and told her to stop. I cried because it made me sad. I thought Grandma was nice, but she's mean. I don't like her!"

"Don't say that Josiah! Grandma loves you. Sometimes grownups say mean things when they are upset. I'm sure she didn't mean it."

"Yes, she did. She said she wished you weren't my mommy because she didn't want a Black grandson. Is being Black wrong? Does that mean she doesn't like me too?"

Oh, my God! I couldn't believe she would say that knowing he could overhear it. Mrs. Michaels never made her dislike for me and people like me a secret. Roger and I dealt with it our entire relationship, but I thought Josiah would change all of that. How could her heart not soften for such a beautiful child? I couldn't let her poisonous views taint Josiah's view of himself.

"There's nothing wrong with being Black, Josiah! It's something to be very proud of. When Grandma was little she was taught that Black was bad, but that is not true. Don't worry about Grandma. We have to love her and...."

"Pray for her."

"That's right."

"I'm going to pray for her and Daddy. Did Daddy go to jail because he's bad, Mommy?"

"Daddy's not bad, but he made a bad choice. Now he has to face the consequences."

"Like when I won't share at daycare and I have to go to time out?"

"Something like that. When you don't follow the rules, you get in trouble."

"I hope Daddy learns his lesson."

"I'm sure he will. Do you want some cookies?" I said, grabbing some butter cookies and changing the conversation quickly.

"Yes, please!" Josiah squealed.

I gave him a few cookies and he forgot all about Grandma being mean and Daddy going to jail. He savored every bite and got lost in his own world. I wished it was that easy for me.

Chapter 3

I was true to my word about not helping Mrs. Michaels bail Roger out of jail. His trial came quickly, within three weeks of his arrest. When I told Georgia, she was devastated and agreed to fast and pray with me until the trial date. Although our relationship was strained, Roger was Josiah's father and I wanted God's will to be done.

Roger and I met at a club. My friend Tanya and I were people watching and sipping on our drinks when he walked up to me. I had never thought about dating outside of my race, but he was the most handsome White man I had ever seen. He had beautiful brown hair that shined like he belonged in a Head and Shoulders shampoo commercial. His green eyes were mesmerizing, and his smile was warm and inviting. His lips were thin, but not too thin like other White boys I had seen. He was dressed neatly in dark jeans, Timberlands and a button-down shirt. I was attracted to him, but decided to play hard to get.

"Hello beautiful. May I have this dance?" he asked and held out his hand.

I laughed in his face, nudged Tanya and walked away.

"He is such a cornball!" I exclaimed loud enough for him to hear.

Despite my behavior, he continued to pursue me. Every Saturday he came to the club, sought me out and asked me to dance the same way. I admired his tenacity so after his fourth attempt I spoke to him instead of laughing in his face and his response changed my life forever.

"What's so beautiful about me?" I asked.

"Your eyes and your smile are breathtaking. I was drawn to you from the moment I saw you. Please dance with me," he said and held out his hand again.

All my young adult life men always complimented me on my figure. No one ever commented on my eyes or smile. I was beginning to think all I had going for me were my hips and behind. The fact that this young man's focus was on something else was impressive to me. I had been so rude. I thought I should give him a chance.

I took his hand as he led me to the dance floor. I was

tense at first, but his gentle touch made me at ease and I melted in his arms. We were so into each other we were still swaying after the last song ended. The DJ announced "You don't have to go home, but you have to get out of here. Yes, I'm talking to ya'll!"

He walked Tanya and me to my car, gave me a quick hug and left. He didn't try to get a feel or beg for my number like the Black men I normally met. I was intrigued to say the least. The next time we saw each other at the club we danced all night again and exchanged numbers. We were connected by the hip until things went downhill after I got pregnant.

Now, I was faced with the fact that Roger may go to prison and be away from me and Josiah for years. I wished it was a dream, but it was very real.

The court room was buzzing with activity. To my surprise, Georgia and Monica joined me. Monica and I had a few conversations after the big blow up and they were tense. She hadn't watched Josiah since then and it was best that way. I decided to forgive and move on, but I would never forget.

They were dressed sharply in black pants suits. Georgia wore a white ruffled blouse with hers while Monica chose a mauve button down. I felt underdressed in my black and white striped shirt and black jeans. We sat quietly three rows behind the defendant's chair. I was in the middle with Monica and Georgia on either side.

There were several cases before Roger's so we anxiously waited for his turn. The bailiff looked bored and uninterested like the day couldn't be over fast enough. His muscular arms and wide chest let us know that he worked out regularly and could easily bring someone down if necessary. I was afraid just looking at him. The court stenographer was typing away quickly with a stern face and her lips pierced together painfully. She wore minimum makeup and her hair pulled back into a tight bun. Judge Campbell's presence commanded order without him saying a word. He was a distinguished looking gentleman with gray hair and a neatly trimmed goatee. His voice was deep, but not overpowering. He spoke in a calm and matter-a-fact tone to each suspect. Some of the cases were absurd, but he took them seriously and treated them fairly.

Soon it was Roger's turn. When I saw him walk into the room, he was unrecognizable. His normally flowing brown hair was dry and lifeless. His eyes were sunken in from lack of sleep and his body looked weak and gangly. He had not shaved so he had a full beard. Wow, three weeks made a world of difference. I had never seen him look so bad. I wished I could give him a hug and comfort him in some way. My heart was broken.

"He looks good, considering," Georgia whispered and squeezed my hand.

Her attempt to ease the shock of his appearance didn't work, but I appreciated her effort. Monica turned and looked at me as if she was searching for something in my face. I gave her a weak smile and turned my attention back to Roger.

He stood before the judge humbly. His usual cockiness was gone and in its place, was respect and fear. He was shaking like a leaf. Roger wasn't afraid of anything or anyone. Where was the tough guy I knew? Where was his fight? It was as if he decided to lie down in the ring and give up before the bell rang. I held my breath as Judge Campbell read the sentence.

"I hereby sentence Roger Michaels to serve a ten-year sentence in Mayfield Federal Prison in Mayfield County, for the distribution of crack cocaine to a minor and distribution of crack cocaine within a five-mile radius of a school. Court adjourned!"

"No! There must be a mistake!" I stood up and yelled.

"Ma'am, please sit down or you will be in contempt of court," demanded Judge Campbell, banging his gavel.

"Roger, how could you do this to our son? How could you?"

"Ma'am, sit down!"

Roger mouthed the words 'I'm sorry' as he was led away and I fell back into my chair unable to control the tears. My head was spinning, and my stomach was in knots.

Georgia and Monica were fanning me with paper, but it wasn't cooling me down.

"Why, Lord? Why, Lord? Oh, my God! Why?" I whispered.

"What do you want?" Monica sneered as Mrs. Michaels approached.

"May I have a word with Maureen?"

"No!" Georgia exclaimed.

"It's okay," I said, thinking Mrs. Michaels and I would have a moment to share in our grief.

"Now that Roger is gone, I don't have to tolerate any more darkies coming in and out of my house. You and your son aren't welcome in my home. Forget you ever met me or my family. Josiah is not my grandson and he is not entitled to anything that comes with that. As far as he's concerned, I'm dead. You can tell him that if you want," she spat.

How could she say that? I thought she loved Josiah. Maybe I read her wrong and there wasn't an ounce of love in her raggedy body. Maybe I saw goodness, where there was none.

I lunged at her ready to wrap my hands around her throat and squeeze her miserable life out of her. Georgia grabbed my hands right before they reached her neck.

"There you go, acting like the animal that you are," she said, looking from me to Georgia and then walked away.

"Let me go, Georgia! Let me go!" I screamed.

"No, Maureen. Don't worry about her. You must think about Josiah. He doesn't need both of his parents in jail," she said calmly.

"It won't matter if his aunt is in there. Let me at her," yelled Monica.

"No, Monica. Vengeance is the Lord's, not ours. It won't do anyone any good to attack her. The Lord will take care of her."

Monica rolled her eyes and sucked her teeth, but she didn't run after Mrs. Michaels.

We left the courtroom in silence. Each of us taking in the day's events in our own way. I believe Georgia was trying to figure out how she was going to help me get through this. Monica was probably thinking about what her friends would say about her sister's baby daddy being in prison. I didn't know what to think. I didn't know what to do next. I didn't know how to tell Josiah, he had lost his father and his grandmother in the same day, but I had to find the words. It would be the hardest conversation I ever had.

My heart was heavy, and I barely had the energy to drive, but when I pulled up to the white brick building with maroon shutters, I smiled. The name of the daycare was Little Hands of Hope. Those words were written on the left-hand side of the building along with a mural of children of different sizes and colors holding hands. I couldn't give up. I had to hold on to hope for Josiah's sake. Roger was in jail and Mrs. Michaels was no longer in the picture, but he still had me.

I was greeted by the sounds of children laughing. It was story time for Josiah's class and the teacher was very animated. Her face lit up as she told the story and the children hung on her every word. I loved all the teachers at the daycare. Most of them knew Josiah from the time he started going there at six weeks old. They were like extra moms and he loved them dearly. They all loved him, but I think the one who loved him the most was the director, Mrs. Calhoun.

Mrs. Calhoun had Josiah's pictures hanging up on the wall in her office and she often declared he was her best friend. She was a lovely lady with salt and pepper hair that she wore in curls. Any room she entered lit up from her presence. She was understanding and went above and beyond to work with me when I had financial struggles. I didn't like to ask to pay late or make payment arrangements, but she was always accommodating. As a first-time mom, I often had questions about parenting and how to handle things with Josiah. She gave me sound advice and didn't make me feel like my questions were silly, although I know they were sometimes. She was like a mother to me and I loved her very much.

"Hi Mama!" she exclaimed when she saw me signing Josiah out. "How are you?"

"Not too good Mrs. Calhoun. I just left court. Josiah's father went to prison," I said with tears in my eyes.

"Oh no! I'm so sorry to hear that!" she said.

"I'm trying to be strong for Josiah, but I don't know how to deal with this. How am I going to tell him, Mrs. Calhoun?"

"I know this is painful, but you can do it. The Lord will give you the right words to say. Josiah is a smart boy. He understands more than you think."

"You're right."

"Josiah Mason, prepare to leave," she said into her walkie talkie.

Moments later Josiah came running around the corner screaming "Mommy"! He ran up to me and gave me the biggest hug possible.

"Boy, you don't even have your stuff. Go get your book bag," I laughed.

"Ok, Mommy!" he said, bouncing away.

"He's something else," I said, shaking my head.

"Call me if you need to talk. I'm here for you," Mrs. Calhoun said, giving me a quick hug.

"I will," I promised.

Josiah came back around the corner with his bookbag and we waved goodbye to Mrs. Calhoun. He filled me in on his day at a mile a minute. His energy was infectious and for a while I pushed thoughts of Roger and his prison sentence out of my mind. Then Josiah's bedtime came, and I had to face the music.

"Mommy, is Daddy home from jail yet?" he asked as I tucked him into bed.

"Not yet, Josiah. Daddy's trouble was bigger than we thought. He's going to be in jail for a long time."

"How long?"

"Ten years."

"That's forever!" he cried and threw the stuffed dog Roger got him for Valentine's Day onto the floor.

"It's a long time, but it's not forever," I said reaching to hug him.

"No, Mommy! No hugs! I'm mad at Daddy. He

doesn't love me!" he yelled.

"That's not true, Josiah. Daddy loves you very much."

"Why did he leave us?"

"He didn't do it on purpose. He would be with us if he could. Daddy loves us, and we will see him again."

"Do we have to go to jail to see him? I don't want to go to jail!"

"You don't have to go to jail, sweetheart. We will figure things out. For now, go to sleep. Here's Buddy back," I said, handing him the dog.

"Is Grandma still mad at you?"

"Grandma doesn't want to be in our lives anymore. We have to keep praying."

"I told you Grandma was mean. God will help her. He's going to help us too, right, Mommy?"

"Yes, He will. We're going to be fine."

"I love you Mommy."

"Sweet dreams, Josiah. I love you too," I said, kissing him on the forehead.

"Good night, Daddy. I love you," he said, hugging Buddy and turning over on his side.

How was I going to help Josiah through this loss and maintain my own sanity? I didn't know, but I had to trust the one who did.

Chapter 4

"What did you say?" I asked Dr. Pearson, my gynecologist for the past ten years.

"You're pregnant, Maureen. Isn't that great!" she said smiling.

"Not really," I said solemnly.

"I know you would rather be married, but a child is still a blessing. Fornication is the sin, not the child. You'll be fine."

Dr. Pearson was a woman of strong faith. She planted seeds of faith in me prior to my accepting Jesus as my Lord and Savior and she had strengthened my walk every time we talked.

She wore her hair cropped short and had the most brilliant smile I had ever seen. Her skin was flawless, and she normally only wore lipstick and eyeliner. She was the reason I decided to wear my natural hair and take pride in it. When referring to a chemical relaxer, she would say "You don't need that creamy crack" and we would laugh so hard we would cry. I never thought of myself as beautiful, but she was an example of beauty that I could look up to and emulate. That was priceless to me.

She was wonderful during my pregnancy with Josiah. Because my father died while I was pregnant, it was harder than normal for me. She went to the funeral and shared an encouraging word. She was much more than a doctor, she was my mentor.

"I know. I'm disappointed in myself because I had been so strong and a moment of weakness has cost me so much. Now, I'm a single parent again and my baby's daddy is in prison."

"What?" she exclaimed.

"Roger was sentenced to ten years in prison a month ago on drug charges."

"I'm so sorry, Maureen," she said hugging me. I knew her feelings were sincere, but I didn't want sympathy. I wanted solutions.

"What am I going to do, Dr. Pearson?"

"You're going to hold your head up high and carry this baby to full term. Then you are going to raise a beautiful God-fearing child."

"What if I can't?"

"You don't have a choice."

"But, I do."

"Are you talking about abortion, Maureen?"

Tears poured down my face as I nodded my head. I couldn't believe I was considering it either. I had always been pro-life, but now that I was faced with an unwanted pregnancy, abortion seemed like the only solution. Josiah was unplanned, but he wasn't unwanted because I was excited to be a mom. This time, I wanted to erase that night with Roger and the baby would remind me of it for the rest of my life.

"As a medical professional, I can discuss the option with you, but as your friend and sister in Christ, I wouldn't recommend it. Don't let your feelings of guilt and shame transfer to this innocent child. This baby is a blessing from God."

"I don't feel blessed right now! I feel like this is a burden I'm going to have to carry for the rest of my life! I'm going to be judged and ridiculed for this. You know how people at Faith Chapel can be. You know how my family is. Why should one mistake have such great consequences? I'm not going to be able to love this child. I'm just going to see guilt and shame when I look at him or her. A mother is supposed to love her child."

"And you will love this child, Maureen. You will," she

said, grabbing my hand.

After a moment, she released my hand and pulled out her Bible. I knew she was going to find a Word perfect for my situation. She was going to give me an answer.

"Psalm 127 verse 3 says, 'Behold, children are a heritage from the Lord, The fruit of the womb is a reward'. You should look at this child as a reward from the Lord, not a curse. This is God's child, not yours. Remember that."

"You're right, but how will I handle the stares and whispers. People already talk about me because I dated a White man and had a bi-racial child out of wedlock. Now they are going to talk about me getting pregnant again by the same man who is in jail on drug charges. It's just too much. I know they are going to question my salvation. I really can't handle that."

"Is that because you've questioned it yourself?" she asked, studying my face.

"I guess so."

"Maureen, the Word says we must work out our own salvation with fear and trembling. Only you know your relationship with Christ. No one can judge that but you and Him. Don't let what other people think bother you. You are a child of God. You must know that and be confident in it no matter what."

"You're right, Dr. Pearson! I love you," I said, hugging her.

"I love you too, Maureen. Now let's talk about this pregnancy and how we are going to make it wonderful and healthy."

The rest of the appointment was filled with information about prenatal vitamins and tips on how to eat healthy and exercise during pregnancy. Dr. Pearson made me feel good about the pregnancy and empowered me to face those that might question my salvation because of it, but when I walked out the door worry and doubt invaded my mind once again. This was going to be the longest nine months of my life!

Not only was my world rocked, but Josiah's was too. He was trying to adjust to life without his father and grandmother and now another change was happening.

We were closer than ever before because it was truly him and me against the world. I didn't know what he would think about being a big brother and having to share me with another child. To my surprise, he was excited. He said the baby was something good happening to us after all the bad stuff. He was right. The baby was a blessing, but everything else going on, not so much.

Chapter 5

The following Sunday at Faith Chapel felt strange. No one knew I was pregnant, of course, but I knew and that was enough to make me paranoid. I felt like people could see the guilt and shame all over me.

The sanctuary at Faith Chapel was filled with music and praise. The congregation consisted of about three hundred faithful members. The pews were made of dark wood and cushioned with bright red velvet. This was for the precious blood of Jesus, we were told almost every Sunday by Pastor Green. He said he wanted to remind everyone that it is Jesus' blood that supports us just like the cushions on the pews. This was profound, but lost most of its thunder the twentieth time I heard it.

The stain glassed windows depicted different scenes from the Bible and each were dedicated to a founding member of the church. There were twelve windows in all, just like there were twelve disciples of Jesus. This was another point, Pastor Green liked to emphasize, but he didn't talk about it as often as he talked about the pews. I especially focused on the scene of Jesus on the cross that Sunday. I knew he died for my sins, but looking at that window made it more real for me than it had ever been before. My sins were forgiven, and I needed to stop focusing on them so much. I was giving them too much power I thought. This made me smile.

"Hello, Sister Mason. It's a fine day, isn't it?" asked Brother Tony Hudson as he sat down next to me.

My heart skipped a beat. He was so fine! I had the biggest crush on him since I joined the church, but I didn't think I was in his league.

I couldn't believe he was sitting next to me. He'd never done that before. I wondered why that day of all days he would do that. Was I giving off some type of vibe because of my pregnancy? I had to put my guard up, but I couldn't help but melt a little as his brown eyes smiled at me. I lost myself in his eyes and was speechless.

"Sister Mason, are you okay?" he asked with a worried look on his face.

"I'm fine Brother Hudson. I'm just basking in the Spirit of the Lord. The music is so wonderful."

"Yes, it is," he said, focusing on the choir.

I was so relieved he wasn't looking at me anymore. I let out a long breath. Relax girl, I said to myself. He's just a man. But, he was a fine, Godly, wonderful man and he was sitting next to me!

He stood up and started to clap his hands to the music. I couldn't help but scan his body with my eyes. He looked so good in his blue pinstriped suit. I turned my head so I would stop lusting. That's what got me into the situation I'm in now I thought. Instead, I focused on what I was there to do, worship the Lord.

During the service, Tony made several attempts at small talk and we shared a Bible. He claimed he was in such a hurry to get out of the house that he left his Bible on the kitchen table, but he wasn't a good liar. I saw it beside him. Why was he trying so hard to be close to me I wondered? Did he think I was a Jezebel? Did he sense it in my spirit? If so, I was going to check him. I wasn't some easy to bed church girl.

"Sister Mason, I have a confession to make," he said at the end of the service.

"What is it?" I asked, anticipating what his response was going to be.

"I didn't leave my Bible at home. It's right here," he said, holding it up.

"Why would you lie Brother Hudson? And in the

house of the Lord?" I said playfully.

Oh Lord, I was flirting with this man in church. Stop it Maureen, I said to myself.

"I know it was stupid, but I didn't know any other way to break the ice with you. You see I have been observing you for quite some time and you seem like the type of lady I would like to get to know better...."

"I'm no Jezebel, Brother Hudson. I don't know what you think...."

"No! It's nothing like that. I've liked you from the moment I saw you join the church, but it wasn't the right time for me to approach you. We both had a lot of growing to do. I believe the Lord has brought us both to the point in Him that it would be okay for us to develop a relationship. I'm not saying let's get married tomorrow or anything. I just want to get to know the beautiful woman of God I know you are and I want you to get to know me," he rambled.

"Are you asking me out on a date, Brother Hudson?" I asked.

"Yes, I am. What do you say?"

"That would be nice," I said as calmly as I could, but my insides were jumping up and down.

"Wonderful. Can we exchange numbers?" he said, grabbing the cell phone that was on top of the Bible he wasn't supposed to have.

We exchanged numbers and said our goodbyes. I was so excited I could hardly stand it. Then the realization that I was carrying another man's child hit me like a ton of bricks. I couldn't go out with him. What was I going to do? I had already told him yes. I needed to talk to Georgia.

On my way to the choir loft, I ran into her husband, Martin, literally.

Martin was a handsome and charismatic man. He had deep brown eyes, curly jet-black hair and was built like a professional basketball player. Georgia was leery when he first asked her out. She thought 'what does a man like that want with a woman like me?' She felt lucky to be with him, but I believed he was the lucky one.

"I'm so sorry, Martin," I exclaimed.

"Where are you going in such a hurry?"

"I was on my way to talk to your wife."

"Did she tell you the great news?" he asked, grinning from ear to ear.

"She told me the two of you were leaving Faith Chapel. I'm sorry to hear that."

"Did she tell you why? I'm being ordained, and we are joining Grace and Deliverance. I will be their Assistant Pastor. Isn't that wonderful?"

I didn't know what to say. I didn't want to lie in church. I said I wanted to talk to him about how his decision was affecting Georgia, so I guess this was my chance.

"I don't think your wife thinks so and neither do I," I said looking him in the eyes.

He grabbed my arm and pulled me away from the crowd. He spoke under his breath, but with an intensity that scared me.

"What my wife thinks is between me and her. How dare you interject your opinion into our marriage! She was upset at first, but she's gotten over it. She knows this is what's best for our family. I would appreciate it if you kept your nose out of our business. Your life is a mess, so you're trying to make ours one too," he growled.

"She told you about...."

"I know you are about to have another baby by that low life White man you've been dealing with. You better stay out of my business if you know what's good for you."

"Are you threatening me? I'm going to tell Georgia."

"You will do no such thing. This is a conversation between me and you. I saw you talking to Brother Tony Hudson. I wonder what he will think when he finds out you're nothing but a whore," he said and let my arm go.

"How dare you talk to me like that! I'm not a whore!" I said a little too loud.

A few people turned our way and began whispering amongst themselves. Just then Georgia walked up and hugged her husband. She saw the stress in my face and my balled-up fists. She knew not to ask me about it right then because I would explode.

"Hey baby," she said to Martin.

"I will talk to you later Georgia, okay," I said marching off without waiting for an answer.

I couldn't believe him. I was not a whore. I just made a mistake, but if he thought that other people might think it too. I didn't know how I was going to deal with that. How was I going to deal with Tony? I couldn't think about that right then. I needed to pick Josiah up from his classroom and go home.

The four and five-year-old classroom was decorated with bright colors and had a mural of the Sesame Street characters on the back wall. Josiah especially loved Big Bird and had to have his room painted yellow because that was the Big Bird color. Seeing the bright colors and the children laughing and playing made me forget about the drama I just left. I looked for Josiah and saw him playing ball with one of the other boys. He was so beautiful. Tears filled my eyes as I thought about how blessed I was that he was my son. I decided I would take him to get ice cream after dinner. He would like that.

"Mommy! Mommy!" Josiah screamed as he ran to me.

I scooped him up and squeezed him as tightly as I could without cutting off his air supply. I put him down and held his hand as I completed the sign out sheet.

"Have a blessed day," I called out to the staff as Josiah and I walked away.

I walked outside and was greeted by the hot summer sun. At least I wouldn't have to suffer through the last months of my pregnancy during the summer like I did with Josiah I thought. My thoughts were interrupted when I heard my name.

"Maureen, Maureen. Wait up," yelled Georgia as she caught up with me.

I really didn't want to talk to her, so I was going to do my best to avoid a conversation.

"I'm in a hurry, Georgia. Can I talk to you later?"

"Hi, Auntie Georgia," Josiah said, smiling at Georgia.

"Hi sweetheart," she said, bending down to give him a hug.

"We have to go Josiah," I said, giving his arm a slight tug.

"What's wrong, Maureen? Why are you so angry?"

Georgia asked innocently.

"Like you don't know," I snapped.

"I don't. Did Martin say something to upset you?"

"How could you tell him about... you know?"

"I didn't tell him anything, Maureen. I swear!" she exclaimed.

"Then how does he know? He said some real ugly and nasty things to me about it."

"He may have overheard one of our phone conversations or something. I haven't told him anything. We don't even talk. I just put on a good front here because I don't want people in our business, but I don't know how much longer we're going to last."

"Are you talking about divorce?"

"We haven't talked about it, but I'm thinking about it."

"I'm sorry, Georgia," I said and gave her a quick hug.

"I'm sorry he was mean to you. I will talk to him about it. He has no right to take his frustration with me out on you."

"I tried to talk to him about your feelings about leaving Faith Chapel, but he didn't want to hear what I had to say."

"You talked to him about what?"

"I just thought maybe I would tell him how leaving

was really affecting you and..."

"I don't need you to speak for me. He is my husband and I can handle my own business," she said glaring at me.

"I was just trying to help, Georgia. That's what friends are for."

"Well, sometimes friends should mind their own business."

"What?"

"You heard me. You've just made things worse."

"What do you mean by that?"

"Don't worry about it, Maureen. Just stay away from Martin and I will make sure he stays away from you. I'll talk to you later. Bye, Josiah," she said, bending down and giving Josiah a kiss on his cheek.

"Bye, Auntie Georgia."

I watched her walk away in shock. I was totally confused. How could I make things worse if she was already thinking about getting a divorce? Why was she so angry with me?

"Let's go, Mommy. It's hot," Josiah, said, tugging on my arm.

"Ok, baby. Let's go eat. Do you want ice cream?"

"Yeah,"

"Okay, we will go to Betty's Ice Cream Shop after

dinner. You can get your favorite."

"Birthday Cake!" he yelled.

"Do you want two scoops or one?"

"Two!"

"Of course, you want two. Come on. Let's run to the car. Ready, set, go!"

Josiah and I ran to the car and pretended like we were about to pass out when we reached our destination. I turned on the air conditioner expecting the air to cool me down. To my dismay, only hot air poured out of the vent. My air was broken again and as always, I didn't have the money to get it fixed. What else could go wrong?

Chapter 6

It had been five days since Tony and I exchanged numbers and he hadn't called. I was beginning to think he had lost interest or maybe he found out about the baby from that big mouth Martin. I wasn't going to call him first.

It was a typical Friday night. I was relaxed and so happy my work week was over.

My job as a customer service representative for an insurance company was very stressful. I was constantly being cursed out and yelled at by some person who felt they were being treated unfairly. It was worth it when I could help someone. That week a customer asked to speak to my manager to give me a compliment. I cherished those moments, especially with all the chaos going on in my life.

I loved the décor in my bedroom. It was like my own

little island paradise. Because I had a great relationship with my landlord and I had been there over four years, he allowed me to paint my walls. They were a beautiful ocean blue and I had a large painting of an island scene over my bed. My ceiling fan was shaped like palm leaves and I loved it. I paid a pretty penny for my bedding. My comforter was off white with gold embellishments and I had matching sheets. I couldn't have the warmth of a lover every night, but at least I could sleep on comfortable sheets.

I was reading my nightly devotional when the phone rang.

"Hi, Sister Mason, it's me, Tony."

"Hi, Brother Hudson" I said dryly. I wondered what excuse he was going to give for just calling.

"I hope it's not too late. I'm sorry it took me so long to call. This has just been a hectic week. My mother fell ill, and they put her in the hospital. She was just released earlier today," he explained.

I instantly felt bad for giving him the cold shoulder and acting childish.

"I'm so sorry to hear that. Is she feeling better?
"What's wrong, if you don't mind me asking?"

"She has ulcers and they were acting up. She doesn't do what the doctors tell her to do. She eats whatever she wants then gets all worked up about simple stuff. I think she learned her lesson this time."

"I hope so."

There was an awkward silence that lasted about 15 seconds, but it seemed like an eternity. I didn't know what else to say.

"Tell me a little about yourself, Maureen. We only know each other from church. I want to know more," he probed.

What was I going to say? I knew what I wasn't going to say.

"Well, I've lived in Crossroads all of my life. I graduated from Crossroads High in 2007. I graduated from Morestead College with a degree in English in 2011. My little man, Josiah is my heart. Do you have any children?" I said way too fast. I felt like I was rambling.

"No, I don't have children, but I would love to have some one day. I went to Morestead too, and graduated the same year. My degree is in Math and I teach at Crossroads High. Small world."

"Yes, it is a small world. I don't know how I didn't know you then. Were you an athlete?" I asked, slowing down the pace. Thank God, the conversation was flowing.

"Yes, I was on the track team. I was into partying and drinking back then. I don't know how I passed some of my classes or performed well at the meets, but God intervened and slowed me down," he explained.

"Won't He do it?" I exclaimed.

"Won't He will!" he responded.

We laughed for about two minutes before we got ourselves together. It was nice to talk to someone who shared the same ideals and sense of humor. We were corny together and it was great.

"I love your laugh," he said in his silky-smooth voice.

"Thank you. I love yours too," I blushed.

"This may seem like an odd request, but can you tell me your salvation story? You can tell a lot about a person by how they came to know the Lord."

"I got saved at my dad's funeral. He had a massive stroke and died suddenly a few months before I had Josiah. He was my only support system because when I got pregnant, my relatives turned their backs on me. I didn't know what I was going to do until I heard the sermon at the funeral. The pastor talked about the unconditional love of Jesus and how we could cast all our cares on Him. I needed to cast my cares somewhere. I had tried everything else, so I figured it was time to try Jesus. I walked up front and my sister Monica came behind me. We both accepted Jesus and started a new chapter in our lives that day. Monica started talking to me again and became a big support for Josiah and me. I know our dad was proud. I wish I would have done it sooner, but it happened in God's time," I explained while tears rolled down my cheeks.

"What an inspiring story, Maureen. It truly happened in God's time. Everything happens for a reason."

"What about your salvation story, Tony?" I asked, thankful to divert the attention away from me.

"My journey with the Lord began at a Christian Student Athletes Group meeting at Morestead. One of my teammates kept asking me to come to the meetings. I told him I wasn't a Christian and I wasn't interested, but he kept asking. Well, one night I was out driving drunk and almost hit an 18-wheeler head on, but I swerved just in time. I ended up in a ditch, but didn't have a scratch on me. There were no broken bones or anything. The crazy thing is I don't remember swerving. People think I'm crazy when I say this, but it was like the car was lifted and placed in the ditch. That's the only way I can explain it. After I walked away from that, I decided there was something bigger than me that helped me, and I needed to know more about it. I attended the meeting and when they asked if anyone wanted to know Jesus as their personal savior I went up. That day changed my life. I will never be the same," he said, his voice cracking with emotion.

"Wow, that's amazing Tony. Our God is a good God!"

"Yes, He is. I'm grateful He allowed our paths to cross."

"Me too."

Every time he made a reference to me and him my face felt like a volcano about to erupt. I didn't know he would have such an effect on me and we were just on the phone. He was intelligent, handsome and a true man of God. He wasn't playing church like so many men I had encountered. Tony was the real deal. I was in awe.

We talked for another hour before we finally said good night. We agreed to meet for lunch the next day at a little diner on the north side of town called Hannah's Heaven. They made the best deli sandwiches and I loved their tea. I told him I would have to arrange for a baby sitter and if I had any problems I would call him to cancel.

"Have a blessed night, Maureen. See you tomorrow."

"I'm looking forward to it. Good night, Tony."

"Good night," he said and hung up.

I couldn't believe I was going on a date with Tony Hudson! I was ready to go, but finding a babysitter was a real issue. Although Monica and I had made up, I still didn't want Josiah to go back to her house. Maybe Georgia would watch him. We hadn't talked since Sunday, but it was worth a try. I said a quick prayer and asked the Lord to give me the words to say. I held my breath as I dialed her number. I truly hoped Martin didn't answer the phone.

"Hello," Georgia answered, sounding like she just ran a marathon.

"Hey, girl. What are you doing?" I asked, letting out my breath.

"I just finished working out. You know I got to keep these curves right!" she said laughing.

She was in a good mood. Thank you, Lord, I thought.

Georgia always embraced her size and didn't try to adhere to the Hollywood beauty standards the media bombarded us with, but lately she seemed more obsessed with exercise. She had worked out in her home gym almost every day for the past month. I wondered if Martin was putting pressure on her to lose weight or something. He never had a problem with her size before, but the way he had been acting lately, I wouldn't put it past him.

"I need to join you. I'm so out of shape..."

"Whatever, Maureen! Your shape is perfect and you know it."

"I don't think so. My thighs have gotten so big and my booty is just out of control. I don't mind having booty, but now it just looks crazy. And it's going to get worse now that I'm pregnant."

"Well, at least being pregnant will give you some breasts. You had it going on with Josiah."

"You're right about that. I just wish everything else would stay as is."

"We don't always get what we want," she said sadly.

"What's wrong, Georgia?"

"Nothing. Just thinking about life and how things have changed. I will be okay. What's up with you? I know you need something. It must be big to make you set aside your pride and call me after we haven't spoken in five days."

"I was afraid you were still angry with me."

"Girl, I got over that Sunday night. You know I'm not one to hold grudges. I've just been busy."

I didn't believe her. She was still angry with me, but she wasn't going to let me know. I decided to let it go.

"Would you like to babysit the best little boy in the whole wide world tomorrow?"

"I guess I can clear my schedule. What do you have going on?"

I didn't want to tell her I was going out with Tony

because I knew she would ask me if I told him I was pregnant. I would say no, and she would lecture me about all the reasons why I needed to tell him. I didn't like lying to Georgia because I usually got caught, but I had no choice this time.

"I'm meeting one of my old college friends for lunch and we will probably hang out for a few hours after that."

"Male or female?"

"Huh?"

"Is this friend male or female?"

My mind raced. Which should I say?

"Female."

"Cool! It's always great catching up with old friends. Just don't forget who your bestie is."

"Never!"

"I know that's right. What time do you want me to pick Josiah up?"

"Around ten will be good. That way I can take my time and get ready without him running around."

"Cool. Ten o'clock it is. I will see you in the morning."

"Thanks, Georgia. Love you."

"Love you too, girl," she said, hanging up the phone.

Chapter 7

I was so excited I couldn't stay still nor be quiet. I got up extra early and took my shower before Josiah woke up. I had thirty minutes to spare so I watched an old episode of "Sanford and Son" on television. I laughed so hard I woke Josiah up before time. He came out of his room in his Spiderman pajamas rubbing his eyes. I felt bad that I woke him up, but he was so sweet looking. I scooped him up and showered kisses all over his face, which he wiped off with his hands. He wasn't very affectionate when he first woke up.

I turned the radio on and sang loudly as I helped him with his bath. I danced around the kitchen as I fixed and served his breakfast. He watched all of this with his forehead wrinkled and his lips turned down in a slight frown.

"Are you okay, Mommy?" he asked.

"Yes, baby. I'm just really happy today."

"Why?"

"Just because. Just because," I answered, kissing him on the cheek.

His eyes narrowed as he weighed my answer. Soon the wrinkles went away, and the frown turned into a smile.

"Ok," he said and sat on the couch to watch his Mickey Mouse Club DVD for the one millionth time.

Georgia rang the doorbell right at ten. I called for Josiah and he met her at the door. I didn't have time for small talk with Georgia. I had to get ready for my dream date with Tony. I told Georgia I would pick Josiah up later and waved them out the door. I knew she thought I was acting strange, but she didn't say anything. I would hear about it later.

Once they were gone, I ran to my closet to pick out the perfect outfit. I was trying to decide between a lavender wrap dress that showcased my curves, or a linen Capri and blouse set when the phone rang. I hoped it wasn't Tony canceling our date.

"You have a collect call from Mayfield Federal Prison. Do you accept the charges?"

It was Roger. I couldn't believe he was calling me. What did he want?

"Do you accept the charges?" the automated voice asked again.

"Yes," I said nervously.

"Hey, baby. What's up?" Roger asked.

"I'm pregnant. That's what's up!" I said before I could stop myself.

"What?" he asked coldly.

"You heard me. Your second child was conceived on that night that meant so little to you."

"How do I know it's...."

"Don't even go there, Roger! You know I had not been with a man in over four years until that night with you. And I haven't been with anyone since. This is your child and you know it."

"So, what you gonna do?"

"I'm keeping it. What do you think? The fact that you're in jail and we aren't together isn't the baby's fault."

"Thank God!" he said with a sigh of relief.

"What?"

"I was calling you to tell you that I'm saved now. I want to make things right with you when I get out."

"Say that again," I said in shock.

"My cell mate is a Christian. He's been locked up for ten years now and has been saved for seven. He led me to

Christ in our cell a couple of weeks ago. I feel so free now, Maureen. I understand what you've been trying to tell me. I guess it took me coming here to see. I know God has forgiven me for all my sins. I just hope you can forgive me one day."

"I can't believe this," I said, shaking my head.

"It's true. Please come see me, Maureen. I need to see you."

"I'll think about it," I said, even though I wanted to say no.

"I have to go. I will write you with the information you need for visitation. I'm going to put you on my list."

"I can't promise...."

"I got to go, Maureen. I love you," he said and hung up the phone.

I stood in the middle of my bedroom floor stunned. My mind was racing. I should have been happy. I had been praying for Roger's salvation for a long time, but now that it happened, it didn't seem real. Could he really change? Did he mean it when he said he loved me or was he just trying to latch onto me, so he could tell his buddies he had a girl waiting on the outside. Plenty of people find God in jail and then forget about Him when they get out. I was so confused. I didn't know how to feel.

Time flew by and it was eleven o'clock and I wasn't

dressed. I quickly chose the lavender dress, put on some eyeliner and lipstick and rushed out the door. I tried to push thoughts of Roger out of my mind and focus on the day ahead with Tony. I wasn't going to let anything ruin this date, especially not myself. I said a quick prayer as I drove down the street.

Lord, help me to focus on the day ahead and not the confusion I feel about Roger. Thank you for saving him and I pray his salvation and newfound relationship with you are real. Help him to grow in you and become the man you intend for him to be. Bless this date with Tony so we can continue to get to know each other better. In Jesus' name. Amen.

I pulled up to Hannah's Heaven about five minutes before twelve. Hannah's was one of my favorite restaurants. They had a cool old school vibe. The pay phone, juke box and waitress uniforms complete with aprons and little checkered hats made me smile. It was like stepping into the TV show Mel's Diner. I often imagined Flo saying, "Kiss my grits!" My mom loved that show and we watched re-runs all the time.

I used to beg Roger to bring me here when we were dating, but he wouldn't because he had issues with the owner. Roger had issues with a lot of people, which should have been a red flag to me, but I didn't want to notice. I shook my head vigorously to shake thoughts of Roger away. I wanted to focus on having a good time with Tony.

When I walked in the diner I spotted Tony already seated at a table by the window. He stood up when I approached, pulled my chair out for me and waited until I was seated before he sat back down. What a gentleman, I thought. He wore a nice pair of jeans and a white, yellow and orange striped polo shirt. His hair was freshly cut and, to my relief; his fingernails were neatly cut without dirt underneath them. Of course, I checked out the shoes. He wore a nice clean pair of white Air Force Ones. I was very pleased with his appearance and he was beyond pleased with mine.

"You look wonderful, Maureen!" he exclaimed.

"Thanks," I said shyly.

"I took the liberty of ordering our drinks when I saw you pull up. I remember you said you loved the tea here, so I ordered one for you. I hope that's okay."

"Yes. Thank you."

I couldn't believe he took the initiative with the drink orders. I never had a man do that for me before. It also proved that he really listened to what I said. I was impressed once again.

"My co-workers and I come here sometimes after work. The school is around the corner," he said.

"So, you really enjoy teaching math? I wasn't the best with numbers when I was in school. Beyond Algebra One, I was lost."

"Yes, I love it. I enjoy working with the ninth graders, but I eventually want to teach at the university level. I'll have to earn my PhD first."

"Well, I know you can do it. You can do all things through Christ who strengthens you!" I said a little too enthusiastically.

"Thank you for the support!" he laughed.

"You're welcome."

"I'm so blessed to have the support of such a beautiful woman," he said staring into my eyes.

I put my head down. I couldn't handle the intensity of his stare.

"You do know that you are beautiful, don't you?" he asked, putting his fingers under my chin and lifting my head.

"Not really," I said honestly.

"Well, you are," he said like it was a fact, not an opinion.

I never thought I was beautiful when I was growing

up. When we were little everyone always complimented Monica on her looks and didn't give me a second glance. It wasn't until I reached my teens and started to develop my curvy lower half that I received some attention, but it wasn't always the right kind.

The waitress came and took our orders and the small talk continued. The more we talked, the more comfortable I became with him.

Everything was going great until I glanced up at the window and saw Monica glaring back at me. She had trouble written all over her face. I thought we were in a good place, but she was geared up to start some drama. She marched into the diner and did just that.

"Hey, Maureen. Won't you introduce me to your friend?" she demanded as she approached the table.

"Tony, this is my sister, Monica. Monica, this is my friend, Tony."

"Nice to meet you, Monica," Tony said, standing up and holding out his hand for her to shake.

Monica looked him up and down, put her hands on her hips and didn't shake his hand. She could be so rude!

"How do you know, Maureen?" she asked, glaring at Tony with the same intensity that she had glared at me through the window.

"We attend the same church," he said, putting his

hand down.

"Oh! You're a hypocrite too!"

"Monica!" I yelled so loudly that the other customers in the diner looked our way.

"What, Maureen? Did I say something wrong?"

"Monica, please stop," I said through clenched teeth.

"Well, Tony, you don't seem like Maureen's type. She likes White thugs. Do you know who her baby's daddy is?"

"Yes. Roger Michaels," he answered.

"Do you know where he is?"

"He's locked up at Mayfield."

"Well, Maureen. I guess you've learned to be more honest these days," she said, looking at me then back at Tony.

"Did she tell you she and Roger were trying to get back together before he got locked up? Word has it she even gave it up," she said calmly like she just said it was a pretty day today.

"Will you please leave, Monica? Stop spreading lies," I said as calmly as I could.

I didn't know what she knew, and I didn't want to set her off. I hadn't told her about the pregnancy because I didn't want a scene just like the one that was playing out before me.

"You must have forgotten that Roger's best friend Man Man's cousin, Lanitra is my girl. She told me everything. Roger bragged to his boys about how he got you to give it up after having it on lock for four years. All he had to do was pretend like he was interested in all the religious stuff you were talking about. You're supposed to be so holy and sanctified. That's a bunch of crap!" she screamed, her face inches from mine.

"Shut up, Monica!" I said as tears fell down my face.

"You are not the one to judge her, Monica. Only God can do that. Let him without sin cast the first stone. What do you gain by coming here and doing this? What if someone did the same thing to you?" Tony asked.

"Look, Tony, you don't know me like that. Don't talk to me about my sister. This is between me and her. I refuse to let her run around town like she's some saint and look down on me," Monica spat pointing her finger at Tony's face.

"Why do you want to hurt me, Monica? I thought we were good? What have I done to you?" I asked through my tears.

"Do you remember the game night you had at your house about three months ago?" she asked.

"Yeah. What does that have to do with this?"

"I heard you and your church friends in your

bedroom talking about me."

"What are you talking about?"

"I heard them saying I wasn't the right type to join the women's fellowship y'all were starting up. They said I was too worldly and I needed to be delivered from this and delivered from that. You agreed with everything they said. You didn't defend me at all. You told them I embarrassed you and sometimes you wished I wasn't your sister. Do you know how much that hurt me? I would never say something like that about you. I tried to move past it, then I heard about you hooking up with Roger and now I see you out with another man. How dare you judge me! How dare you!" she said, tears pouring down her face.

She must have found out I slept with Roger the same night it happened. That's why she was so upset when I picked Josiah up. That explained a lot, especially her reference to things coming to light. I didn't know what to say. Apologizing was the best I could do.

"I'm sorry, Monica," I said.

"Sorry you said it or sorry I heard you?"

"Both."

"Well, save it! The damage is done. You don't have to worry about me anymore. You have your wish. I'm not your sister, okay!" she yelled and ran out of the diner.

I didn't know she heard that conversation. I did say sometimes I wished she wasn't my sister, but I didn't mean it. It was a joke. Right after I said it, I told the ladies that it wasn't true. No matter how much we fussed, fought and embarrassed one another, she was always going to be my sister and I loved her. Of course, she didn't hear that part. I never should have said it, but I couldn't take it back now. That slip of the tongue may have cost me my relationship with my sister.

"Are you going to run after her?" Tony asked.

"No. There's no use," I said defeated.

"You sure?"

"Yeah. I think I'm going to leave."

"Please don't go."

"You still want to continue this date after all of that?"

"We shouldn't let your sister ruin our time together."

"You don't care about the things she said?"

"Like I told her, I can't judge you. That's the Lord's job. We all fall short of the glory of God. It's whether we get back up that's important."

"Thank you for being so understanding, Tony, but I don't think I can stay."

The waitress came up and placed our orders on the table. She looked at me and shook her head before walking away.

"I can't eat. I'm too upset. I will pay for it," I said, reaching into my purse.

"That's okay. It won't go to waste. Don't worry," he said, putting his hand up to motion me to stop.

"I'm sorry, Tony. Maybe I'll see you in church tomorrow."

"Okay. Have a good day, Maureen," he said clearly disappointed.

"Bye," I said and left.

Chapter 8

Why was this happening to me? I was pregnant by a prisoner, embarrassed out of my mind in front of the man I liked and may have lost my sister forever. She was all I had.

When our mother died, I tried to be a good example for her and be the best big sister I could be. I felt like I failed her when I hooked up with Roger and got pregnant. Then when our father died, I was lost and scared and had to depend on her. I was so hurt. I didn't know which way to go because I no longer had parents to guide me, so I clung to my sister. An ill spoken word may have ruined that relationship forever.

Suddenly, I heard a knock on my car window. It was Tony. How long had I been sitting there like a crazy person?

"Are you okay?" I heard him ask as I rolled down the window.

"Yes. I will be fine. The situation just now was so overwhelming. I just have to get myself together," I mumbled.

"Are you sure?"

"Yes. Don't worry. Thank you for everything. Have a good day," I said and rolled the window back up.

He stood there and stared at me for a while and then walked back into the diner. He was so sweet and concerned. I didn't deserve anyone that nice. I was too messed up.

I dried my tears and pulled away from the diner. I needed to pick up Josiah, go home and lie down. I thought a nap would make me feel better and help me to settle my thoughts and figure out what to do next.

Martin and Georgia had a beautiful home. It was a brick four bedroom, two and a half bath home in the Cedar Hills subdivision, where most of the affluent Black people lived. Martin owned his own graphic design business and Georgia was the district manager for a major department store. From the outside, they had the perfect marriage and the perfect life, but based on recent events, I knew trouble was brewing. When I walked up to the door, I could hear yelling. I stood still and listened for a moment, so I would know what I was walking into.

"What is your problem, Georgia? You can't do

anything right!" Martin yelled at the top of his lungs.

"I don't know what you want me to do, Martin! I'm not perfect. I can't be what you want me to be."

"You can, and you will! I have not worked this hard to reach this place for you to mess it up for me. You will be the perfect Assistant Pastor's wife, if it kills me!"

"Well, it may have to kill you because I'm not this perfect little mousy preacher's wife. I have opinions of my own and I'm not going to let you or anyone else tell me how to act or what to do!"

"All you had to do was go to the prayer breakfast, be quiet and eat. What's so hard about that?"

"I had to watch Josiah and you told me about it last night. You were at the prayer breakfast. What's the problem?"

"My wife is supposed to attend functions like that with me. It doesn't look good for me to be there alone. Everyone was asking me where you were. It was so embarrassing!"

"Well, I'm sorry. You should have just told them I had another engagement."

"Watching this kid for that wild girlfriend of yours is not another engagement. I don't see why you hang with her anyway. She's nothing but a whore!"

"Don't you dare talk about Maureen like that! We

all make mistakes. You should know about that."

"What's that supposed to mean?"

"I wonder how your new church family would feel if they knew about Tyra!"

Who was Tyra? I had never heard Georgia talk about someone named Tyra before.

"Don't you bring her into this!"

"You brought her into this a long time ago. I think she's here to stay, but you don't want to own up to it."

"I don't want to talk about this anymore, Georgia. Don't you ever say that name again. She has nothing to do with this situation," he said lowering his voice.

"Oh, don't get quiet now! You were screaming and stomping earlier, but as soon as it comes out that you are not perfect, you don't know how to handle it! Well, you are not perfect! You want to be Assistant Pastor because of what you think it can do for you, but you don't understand what you have to do for it!"

There was a brief silence and then I heard Josiah cry.

I knocked on the door and waited for someone to open it. When they didn't answer, I knocked louder.

"Hey, Georgia. It's Maureen. I've come to pick up Josiah. Let me in," I called out as calmly as I could.

Georgia opened the door with this fake smile on her face. Josiah ran to me and hung on for dear life.

"What's wrong, Josiah?" I asked, searching his face.

"I'm ready to go, Mommy."

"I'll walk you to the car, Maureen," Georgia said, walking out of the door. I noticed she was holding her arm funny, but I decided not to ask her about it.

"Are you okay, Georgia?" I asked, knowing she wasn't.

"Yes, I'm fine. Josiah and I had a lot of fun, didn't we little man?"

"Yes ma'am," Josiah said not looking at her.

"Your lunch ended early?"

"It's a long story. I'll tell you later. See ya," I said and hugged her goodbye.

She jumped a little when I hugged her. I think I may have hurt her arm. I planned to call her later to get the real story.

"Are you hungry, Josiah?" I asked as we drove away.

"I want some fries."

"Okay, fries it is."

Because I didn't eat the food at the diner, I was starving. I went through a drive thru restaurant, purchased a chicken nugget combo for me, a small order of fries for Josiah and we went home.

I was so glad to settle down in front of the couch and watch Mickey Mouse with Josiah. I forgot about the drama of the day for a moment and just enjoyed time with my son. Soon I would be sharing these moments with another child. I loved Josiah so much, I didn't know if I would have enough love to go around. People had more than one child all the time and it works out, but sometimes one child feels less love than the other. I always felt my mother loved Monica more than me and when we grew up, Monica always felt like my father loved me more. I guess it's all a matter of perception. Parents just do the best they can.

I was ready to turn in soon after dinner and luckily Josiah was as well. After his bath, I read a Bible story to him and kissed him good night. I was about the turn the lights off when he reminded me of something very important.

"Mommy, aren't we going to say our prayers?"

I really didn't feel like praying. I felt like God was so disappointed in me that He really didn't want to hear from me, but Josiah needed to speak to Him, so I agreed.

"Dear Lord, please bless Mommy, Daddy, Grandma Michaels and Aunt Monica. Bless my teacher and my friends at daycare. And please Lord; make Uncle Martin stop hurting Auntie Georgia. Amen."

"What do you mean, Josiah? What did Uncle Martin do to Auntie Georgia?"

"Today he grabbed her and hurt her arm. I was so scared. He told me I better not tell you, but I thought it was okay to tell Jesus. I can tell Him anything, right?"

"Yes, Josiah. You can tell Jesus anything. I'm so sorry you saw that, and you were scared. I knew something was wrong."

"I don't like it when they yell. They always yell when I'm there. Is it because of me? Is it because they don't like me?"

"No, baby, it's not your fault. Auntie Georgia and Uncle Martin love you very much. Grownups just yell sometimes when they are angry. Aunt Monica and I yell sometimes, but we still love each other," I said, hoping things were not over for me and Monica.

"Not like Uncle Martin and Auntie Georgia yell. I hate it. It makes me cry. I don't want to go back. Do I have to go back, Mommy?" he asked hugging my neck.

"No, baby, you don't have to go back," I said squeezing him tight.

"I love you, Mommy," he said and laid back down in the bed.

"I love you too. Now let's go to sleep," I said, kissing him again and turning off the light.

I couldn't believe it. Georgia and Martin were arguing and yelling around Josiah and not thinking about how it was affecting him. Then, he witnessed Martin hurting Georgia. My poor baby! Poor, Georgia! I doubt today was the first time. Why didn't I see the signs? What kind of friend was I?

I was a horrible sister, a horrible friend and a horrible Christian. Martin should have been asking what's wrong with me. Who's Tyra? So much was going through my mind. I didn't know what to do. I couldn't confront Georgia because she would deny it and probably get angry with me. I couldn't confront Martin because then he would know Josiah told me. I couldn't yell or scream because the sound was stuck in my throat. I couldn't pray about it because I was unable to form the words. All I could do was cry. Crying didn't do anything to help the situation, but tears didn't need sound. Tears just flow. Crying doesn't take a lot of energy. It doesn't take a lot of thought. Crying is just crying. I cried myself to sleep.

The next morning, I awoke to Josiah hitting my arm. I looked at the clock and it was eight o'clock.

"Mommy, wake up. Are we going to church today?" he asked.

"No, sweetie. Mommy doesn't feel good. No church today. Are you hungry? I'll make you some cereal and you can watch one of your videos until I get up, okay," I said rolling out of bed.

"Okay," he said and ran out the room.

I just couldn't bring myself to go to church. I couldn't face Tony, Georgia and Martin. There was just too much drama going on for me to handle. I fixed Josiah some cereal and sat it on his kiddie table, so he could eat in front of the TV. Surprisingly, he didn't want to watch Mickey Mouse. Instead, he asked me to find a church service for him to watch. He said he wanted to watch church since he couldn't go. I flipped the channels until I found T.D. Jakes. Joel Osteen came on afterwards so that would keep him occupied for a while. I laid back down, but I couldn't go back to sleep. I just thought about the past couple of months and how my life was so out of control. How could I let things get like this? I was in deep thought when the phone rang.

"Hello."

"Hi, Maureen. It's Tony."

Why was he calling me? I couldn't deal with this right now.

"Hi, Tony."

"I was trying to catch you before you left for church. I wanted you to know that I'm still interested in getting to know you. I know you were upset when you left the diner yesterday."

"I don't think that's a good idea, Tony. I have a lot

going on right now."

Tony was the last person on my mind. Worrying about Josiah, the baby, Monica and now Georgia was already more than I could handle.

"Me too. Maybe we could help each other. I really enjoyed the time we did spend together. You shouldn't let your sister's outburst ruin our thing."

"I didn't know we had a thing," I said a little too harshly.

"You know what I mean, Maureen," he stammered.

"I'm sorry if I'm being rude. I just have a lot on my mind. Can we talk another time?"

"Sure. I will see you later in church."

"I'm not going to church this morning, so you don't have anything to worry about."

"Are you okay?"

"I just don't feel well. I will talk to you later, okay."

"Okay. Bye, Maureen."

"Bye," I said and hung up.

I didn't like being mean to him, but I had no choice. I didn't want to talk and that was the best way to get him off the phone. I was irritated and wanted to be left alone. I almost screamed when the phone rang again.

"What?" I yelled into the phone.

"What a way to answer the phone! What's wrong with

you?" Georgia asked.

"Nothing. Sorry."

"Your hormones messing with you already?" she laughed.

"What do you want, Georgia? I'm not in a good mood this morning."

"I can tell. I just wanted to make sure you were alright. You seemed upset when you left yesterday."

"I should be asking you that. I noticed you were holding your arm. Did you hurt it?"

She paused for a moment. I suppose she was trying to think of a good lie. I waited patiently to see what she was going to come up with.

"Yes, I'm fine. I tripped on the rug on the way to the door and fell. You know I can be so clumsy," she laughed.

"Yes, you can. So that's why it took you so long to get to the door?"

"Yes. Why the third degree, Maureen?"

"I'm not giving you the third degree, Georgia. I'm just asking questions. Why? Do you have something to hide?"

"Of course not! You are tripping, girl. I wanted to let you know that I can't do dinner with you after church today because Martin has a speaking engagement this afternoon at Church of the Disciples."

"That's cool. I'm not going to church today anyway."

"Really? Why not?"

"I don't feel good, Georgia. I just need to stay home and relax."

"Oh. Okay. I guess I'll holler at you later," she said hesitantly.

"Okay, bye," I said, hanging up the phone.

She was not a good liar. Why would she feel the need to lie to me? I was her best friend. She could tell me anything. I had to figure out a way to get her some help without letting her know that I knew. How could I do that? It seemed impossible. My thoughts were interrupted by Josiah clapping and singing in the living room. He was singing "I Am a Friend of God" by Israel and New Breed and sounded so sweet.

The only two words I understood were friend and God, but he was throwing down. I felt so blessed to have a child that loved the Lord and church the way Josiah did. I wished I still had his enthusiasm.

We spent the rest of the day hanging out at home. I watched Lifetime Movies and cried all day and Josiah played with his toys between watching various DVDs. I threw myself into the lives of the women on television. Some of their circumstances were worse than mine and it was comforting to see that they survived.

Chapter 9

I drifted through the next few weeks like a zombie, going through the motions of work and taking care of Josiah, but having no idea how I accomplished anything. I was afraid to talk to Monica and avoided Georgia like the plague. I didn't go to church service or Bible study and ignored Tony's texts and phone calls telling me what I missed and how much he missed me. I didn't want to be missed. I just wanted to be left alone. I was a shell of my former self trying to maintain my sanity.

After a particularly rough day at work, all I wanted to do was take a nice warm bath and bury myself in my covers. I wished I could stay there forever, but that wasn't an option. I had to press forward for me, Josiah and the baby.

I stopped by the mailbox on the way home and was shocked to see a letter from Mayfield Federal Prison.

I was excited and scared at the same time. I wanted to know how Roger was doing, but I was afraid of what he would say about us and the baby.

Where did the thought of "us" come from? Was there such a thing as us? Things were not going anywhere with Tony and me after the diner incident. Maybe there was a chance for Roger and me to pull things together. Josiah and the baby needed us.

I still loved Roger despite everything, but I wasn't sure he was what I wanted. Was I settling because he's my kids' father? Was there more out there for me? If someone like Tony could take interest in me, maybe there were better options, but the pickings were slim for a single mom with two kids. Oh, my God! I was thinking way too much about this. It's not that serious Maureen, I thought to myself. It's just a letter.

"Mommy, why are we still sitting here? I'm ready to go home," Josiah, said breaking my thoughts.

"I'm sorry, baby. We're going home," I stammered. I shook my head as if doing so would clear out the guck going on inside of it.

I decided to wait until Josiah was in the bed before I read the letter. After taking several deep breaths, I opened it with the same nervousness of a high school student opening a letter from their top college pick. I was hoping for good news.

Dear Maureen,

I know I promised to write earlier, but our privileges were taken away a couple of days after our phone call. We finally got them back today.

First, I want to apologize for being such a jerk. I admit that my only goal that night was to get you to have sex with me. I had been planning it for months. I wanted to prove that you weren't the saint you wanted everyone to think you were. I shouldn't have come at you like that. I missed your body and I wanted it, but I didn't think about your feelings. I could tell it wasn't something you were proud of when it was going down, but I didn't care. I wanted to prove a point. Please forgive me Maureen. I asked Jesus to forgive me and I hope you have enough love in your heart to forgive me too.

I know I haven't been the best father to Josiah and by the time I get out of here he will be a teenager, but I want him to know how much I love him. I don't want him to see me like this until he's old enough to understand. I will let you decide when that is. Until then, I would like to send him letters and drawings. He always loved for me to draw pictures of Mickey Mouse and things like that for him. Please share the letters with him when the time is right. I don't want prison bars to keep me from my son's heart.

Please come see me. I thought I could just add you to the list, but you must complete the enclosed application. Please fill it out and mail it back to me as soon as you can.

I love you Maureen. Please believe that.

Always,
Roger

P.S. – My cellmate started a Bible study here and I'm learning so much. It's like everything you tried to tell me makes sense now. I guess I'm finally ready to listen.

I couldn't believe what I had just read. Roger admitted he manipulated me and purposely wanted to discredit my salvation. How dare he attack me on such a deep level! Then after all of that he had nerve enough to say he loved me! All the anger, tension and stress I had been feeling lately was because of him and his ego. I knew hate was a strong word, but at that moment I hated Roger Douglas Michaels!

When Roger and I first broke up I hated him with a passion. If he was on fire, I wouldn't have spit on him. I would literally get nauseous every time someone said his name; I heard his voice or laid eyes on him. It wasn't until Josiah turned three and he started to spend more time with his son that I slowly let go of the pain. I realized that I had to forgive Roger for myself. My blood pressure was elevated, and I was having migraines, so it was starting to affect my health. I wasn't going to let anyone cause me to shorten my life span. I had a child to think about. Forgiving him was the best thing I could do for myself and Josiah, but at that moment all the forgiveness was thrown out of the window. How could I allow myself to get sucked back into his world of pipe dreams and empty promises?

The more I thought about it the more I realized how calculated his plan was. After he began to take more of an interest in Josiah and appeared to be trying to put his life in order, I let my guard down. It started out with longer phone conversations about things other than Josiah. Then we started meeting for lunch once a week and I would let him come into my apartment for a little while when he dropped Josiah off. Eventually he would come by when Josiah was spending the night away from home and we would spend hours laughing, talking and studying the Bible. Finally, he started spending the night, at first on the couch, then in my bed. Fooling around turned into going "all the way" and now we are having baby number two. How could I be so stupid?

I ripped the letter and visitor's application into pieces and threw them into the trash can. I pulled out a photo album that had pictures of us when we were dating, grabbed a pair of scissors, took various pictures out of the album and started cutting until my hands ached. Soon I got frustrated, threw the album on the floor and threw myself on my bed.

What was I doing? I couldn't let him upset me like this. I had to think about the baby. I couldn't allow him or her to come into a world where their mom was crazy with rage. I didn't want to live like that again. I couldn't let this consume me.

Roger was a non-factor in my life from that day forward. Yes, he was the male who helped create my beautiful children, but he was no more and no less than that. I needed to get myself together. I always felt better when I prayed. I hadn't done it in a while, but that moment seemed like the perfect time to yield to my Father.

Dear Heavenly Father, I come before you tired and

exhausted. Life is way too hard right now. I can't deal with all of this by myself. I need your help. I need your guidance. Please show me the way. Please help me. I Peter 5:6-7 says I should humble myself under your mighty hand and cast all my cares onto you. You will exalt me in due season because you care for me. I'm casting everything upon you right now Jesus. It is too heavy of a load for me to bear. I praise you in advance for the victory. In Jesus' name. Amen.

I drifted off to sleep while praying into my tear drenched pillow. I dreamed of a hand lifting me up toward heaven and taking away all the baggage I was carrying. What a beautiful dream it was.

Chapter 10

The next morning, I felt a renewed sense of peace. I was wearing my superwoman cape and standing on top of the world. Avoiding Monica and Georgia was no longer an option. I needed to face them head on.

I decided to address Monica first. We hadn't seen each other since the diner fiasco and the anger was still brewing. I went to her house after work and prayed she would accept my apology.

When I pulled up to her house this time, I took the time to really admire what my sister had accomplished. She was so proud the day she closed on her house. She used some of Daddy's insurance money for her down payment and got a great rate. She wanted me to buy the house next to hers, but I declined. I made some bad financial choices, so I used my money to pay down debt and prepare for Josiah instead.

I held my breath as I rang the doorbell because I didn't know what side of Monica I was going to meet.

"Who is it?" she asked from the other side of the door.

"It's Maureen, Monica. Can I come in?"

"What do you want?" she asked with much attitude.

"Open the door and find out please."

She flung the door open forcefully and glared at me like she did that day at the diner. This was not going to go well.

"Come on in. I'm in the kitchen," she said and lead the way to her state of the art kitchen.

It was a chef's dream. Monica loved to cook and wanted to be an executive chef at a five-star restaurant. She was selling cookware to earn money for culinary school because she wanted to be able to pay for it straight out and be debt free. She was one of the top sellers in her company because she could turn off the crazy and turn on her professional demeanor in the blink of an eye. It was scary how she could tell someone off in one breath and then a couple of minutes later deliver a fantastic presentation. Crazy Monica was front and center that day and Professional Monica was nowhere to be found. I thought maybe I could bring her out.

"How was your day? Mine was crazy." I said

pleasantly as I sat on one of the stools around her marble island.

"I don't have time for small talk Maureen. What is it?" she said, rolling her eyes.

"I'm pregnant!" I blurted out.

"And?" she asked with irritation in her voice.

"What do you mean, and?"

"And tell me something I don't know. I found out the day after you told Roger. You keep forgetting about Lanitra. She keeps me in the loop with everything going on with you, especially since you don't."

"Oh. I didn't want you to find out that way. I wanted to tell you first."

"Really? Then how come Roger, his friends and everybody in the hood knew before me!"

"What?"

"Don't play dumb, Maureen. Crossroads is not that big. Roger called one of his boys right after he got off the phone with you. The word spread like crazy. No one wanted to tell me because they knew I would be upset, but Lanitra had my back and let me know the next day. Even Aunt Mattie called me to confirm. I was like 'Yeah it's true, but I didn't get it from her'. I was waiting to see how long it would take for you to come clean with me. I can't believe it took you a month."

"Aunt Mattie knows?" I asked in shock.

Aunt Mattie was our mother's older sister and she lived around the corner from our old house. I hadn't seen Aunt Mattie in months. I knew she was disappointed to hear I was pregnant again and then to find out on the streets instead of from me. I had to make things better.

I should have known once Roger knew it was going to get to his friends and ultimately to Monica. She was right that it shouldn't have taken me a month, but why would I tell her anything after the way she treated me?

"Yes. Aunt Mattie knows. I looked like a fool with everyone hearing this news before me."

"Well, I think you forgot one detail. The last time we saw each other you told me I wasn't your sister anymore and you were very angry. Why do you think I would have told you anything?"

"Because you know I didn't mean that. We will always be sisters, no matter what. You hurt me bad Maureen and you needed to know how much. You owe me an apology."

I didn't want to admit it, but I did owe her an apology for even more than the unfortunate conversation with my church members.

"I do regret that you heard my comments and were upset. If you would have kept listening, you would have heard me tell the ladies it was a joke because no matter how much we fuss and fight you are my sister and I love you. But I need to apologize to you for so much more.

After we got saved, I became a super Christian. I was on fire for Jesus and wanted everyone to know it. Looking back, I think I may have been too forceful with you. I wanted you to dress like me, act like me and live like me. I aimed for perfection and felt you should too. You are not perfect, and neither am I. I admire your freedom to be yourself and not conform to what other people think you should be. You wear what you want, praise the Lord the way you want and don't hold your tongue for anyone. I really admire that. I'm too busy worrying about what others think to be myself most of the time. I don't know if I even know who I am, but I know that I love you. Please forgive me," I said, reaching out to her for a hug.

She fell into my arms and held me tight. It was like she had been waiting all her life for that hug. Or maybe it was for what I said. Either way I was thankful.

"You will never understand what those words mean to me. I know I ain't the best sister and I always make you mad, but I really do love you, Maureen. I apologize for the way I acted at Hannah's. I was just so mad. It really hurt me that you slept with Roger, then I see you on a date with another man shortly after. I was like, is this my sister or some whore? I know that's harsh, but it's what I was thinking. Then I found out you were pregnant and knew it when you were on that date. I was done! I really had to pray about that thing. I had to forgive you and realize it wasn't my job to judge you, but to love you."

"Yeah, that's harsh, but I understand how it looked and how you felt. I'm sorry I disappointed you. I try to set a good example, but I make mistakes too," I said as tears flowed down my face.

"I don't feel like that anymore. I don't understand what you've done, but I understand that it's not my place to understand it. I hope that makes sense."

I nodded yes. She was really impressing me with her insight and how mature she was behaving. I had underestimated my baby sister.

"I need to apologize for how I treated Josiah. I love my nephew. His skin color or lack of color has nothing to do with that. Please accept my apology, Maureen."

"I accept your apology Monica and I'm so glad you accepted mine. We've come a long way from those bickering little girls who used to get on Daddy's nerves. I think he would be proud."

"Yes, he would," Monica said, smiling for the first

time since she opened the door for me.

"Next time, let's talk things out instead of lashing out at each other. It isn't a good look," I said, kissing her on her cheek.

"Go ahead with all of that," she said playfully pushing me away.

"So, we're good?"

"Yes, we're good until we fuss about something else." Monica laughed.

"Yep. That's what we do."

"That's what sisters do."

"Exactly."

"I will be right back." Monica said and left to go into her bedroom.

She came back with a huge gift bag and handed it to me.

"Here are some things I got for Josiah last week. It's not much, some clothes and toys."

"Wow! You sure spoil your nephew! Thanks, hun. Hopefully you will spoil your new nephew or niece too."

"Niece would be nice."

"Yes, it would." I smiled.

I enjoyed having a boy, but a girl would be wonderful. My focus was to have a healthy baby. That's what I wanted more than anything.

"Okay sis. I really need to get ready for this party. Please call Aunt Mattie when you get a chance. No worries. I got your back. Let me know about your next appointment so I can go," Monica said giving me a quick hug.

"Will do, sis. Love you." I said, hugging her back.

She walked me out the door and I was on cloud nine when I left. I was so glad we talked. Everything was out in the open about the baby. I would have a lot of fallout to deal with, but with Monica by my side, I knew I would get through it. My cell phone rang, and it was Georgia. I thought it was great timing since I planned to call her next.

"Hi Maureen, are you busy?" Georgia asked.

"I'm on my way to pick Josiah up. I am just getting ready to call you to see if we could meet. Our last conversation wasn't good, so I really want to talk and clear the air."

"Now isn't a good time for that conversation, but I need your help. Can you pick me up from the emergency room after you get Josiah?" she asked quietly.

"The ER! What's wrong?" I exclaimed.

"I fell down the stairs in front of the house and hurt my head and arm. They say I have a concussion and a broken arm, so I have a cast. Chile, this pain medicine has me so high I can't drive. I'm a mess!" she said, giggling and talking too fast.

"That doesn't sound funny at all Georgia! Did Martin have anything to do with this?" I asked. I knew she was going to be mad, but I needed to know.

"No! Of course not!"

"Stop lying Georgia! I know he hurt your arm the other day. I could hear you arguing and then Josiah screamed. I saw right through your slipped on the rug lie. You don't have to lie to me. I can help you." I pleaded.

"I'm not lying Maureen. I...."

"I'm coming Georgia. I will see if Mother Holmes can watch Josiah and I will be there as quickly as I can. Okay?"

"Okay. I'm sorry Maureen," she said, her voice cracking.

"No worries. I got you. I will call you when I'm on the way."

"Okay."

I picked Josiah up from daycare and called Mother Holmes on the way home. She was a sweet lady in her late 60s who was still foxy and full of life. She wore her long gray hair pulled back in a braided ponytail. She loved to crotchet, cross-stitch and watch reality TV. She knew more about The Real Housewives of Atlanta than I did. We connected instantly when Josiah and I moved in next door to her. She was the only neighbor who welcomed us and made us a delicious pound cake.

She lived alone and her children and grandchildren only came by when they needed something. They never spent any real time with her or took her out. I adopted her as my mom and Josiah's grandmother and we looked out for her.

We loved movie nights with her on the weekends. We would bring the movie and popcorn and she would make something sweet like a cake or cookies. She loved Josiah and had watched him before, but I didn't ask her often because I didn't want her to feel like I was taking advantage of her kindness.

"Hello Mother Holmes. Are you busy?" I asked when she answered the phone.

"Of course not." she laughed.

That was our private joke because whenever anyone asked her if she was busy she would always say "of course not" even if she was. I always knew if she was busy or not by the tone she used when she said it. This time she really wasn't busy.

"I need a big favor. Can you watch Josiah for me? I need to pick a friend up from the hospital?" I asked.

"The hospital? Oh no! Praise Jesus, they will be

alright. Bring him on." she said. I could picture her lifting her holy hands in the air when she said, "Praise Jesus" and it made me smile.

"Thanks. I will be right over. I have some leftover spaghetti. I will bring enough for both of you for dinner."

"Well, thank you, sweetheart. I haven't cooked today, so that will be great."

"Okay. See you soon." I said and hung up.

"Who's in the hospital, Mommy?" Josiah asked.

"One of Mommy's friends, Josiah." I said.

"Praise Jesus, they will be alright!" he said and lifted his hands above his head.

"Thanks baby." I laughed. My little man was something else.

I rushed into the house, used the bathroom, told Josiah to go as well, put the spaghetti in a large bowl and rushed back out. Mother Holmes showered us with hugs and kissed and prayed with me before I left. I didn't know what I was going to encounter, but I knew Jesus would work it out.

Chapter 11

My mind was racing a mile a minute as I hurried to the hospital. I called Georgia to let her know I was on the way, but my call went straight to voicemail. Panic gripped me, and I couldn't breathe. What if Martin beat me there and had already picked her up? I couldn't let her go back to that situation.

Lord, please protect Georgia and keep her safe. Please let her be there when I arrive so she can get the help she needs. Keep Martin far away from her. Help him to understand the error of his ways so that he can learn how to express his feelings without physical violence. He needs to be healed from whatever wounds are causing him to lash out this way. She needs to be healed from the mental, emotional and physical wounds he has caused. Help her to love herself enough to get out of this relationship and realize that she is worth so much more. Help me to be there for her and help her through this process. In Jesus' name. Amen.

When I arrived, I wasn't prepared for what I saw. Georgia had more than just a bump on her head and a cast on her arm. Her left eye was swollen shut and her right eye was black and blue. Her lips were bleeding and she was holding an ice pack on them. When she saw me, she burst into tears and I held her tight. My God, my God, why was this happening? Not my sweet Georgia.

I pulled her away from me and looked into her swollen eyes. Not only could I see the pain, but I felt it as well. I would have given anything to take it away.

"It's going to be okay." I whispered.

We both cried as she put her head on my shoulder and I rocked her like a baby. Time stood still until we were interrupted by a familiar and terrifying voice.

"Come on baby. Let's go home." Martin said with such sugary sweetness it made me nauseous.

I looked up at him with all the hate and contempt my eyes could muster. How dare he speak to her? How dare he be here?

"Get away from her! She isn't going anywhere with you!" I yelled as loud as I could.

"She's going to be fine Maureen. She just needs to be more careful. You can leave now."

"She's not going anywhere! She's going home with me, not you!"

"Don't be ridiculous. She...."

"How about you both stop talking about me like I'm not here! I can speak for myself." Georgia said with a strong voice.

"That's right baby. Come on home." Martin said and reached for her.

"Don't touch me!"

A security guard intervened at that moment and instructed Martin to leave. Martin was resistant at first, but when the guard threatened to call the police he relented. His eyes widened and darted back and forth like a cartoon villain until they settled on Georgia. He stared at her until she began to shake, then he walked away.

"It's okay Georgia. He won't hurt you again. Don't worry." I tried to reassure her.

"No, it's not okay. He's going to kill me," she cried.

"No, he's not. The devil is a liar. I won't let anything happen to you."

"I can't go home with you Maureen. He will find me there and possibly hurt you or Josiah," she whispered.

"Okay. We will find somewhere for you to go. I'm here to help with whatever you want to do."

We were referred to a shelter in a remote section of town. Because we didn't know whether he had tracker software on her phone, she turned it off and left it at the hospital. I would pick it up later.

Safe Haven for Women was a converted motel. The lobby area was beautiful with mahogany hardwood floors and sea green walls. The walls were covered with photographs of women in various positions of worship. One lady was stretching her arms towards heaven while another was on bended knees with her hands in the prayer position. We were told that they were portraits of previous residents. A professional photographer donated his time and equipment to photograph the women during their last week. On their last day, he presented a framed photograph to the woman and Safe Haven. His only instruction was for the women to pose in the position that makes them feel free. All these women felt free in worship. They were praising God for breaking the bonds of abuse and allowing them to walk into a new life. I felt tears fill my eyes as I gazed into their eyes and tried to imagine the freedom they felt.

"Your photo will be up there one day, Georgia. You're going to be free," I said as we walked arm in arm past the photos.

"I don't know what freedom means Maureen. I feel like it's been beaten out of me," she said squeezing my arm tighter.

I didn't know what to say. There wasn't anything for me to say. I wasn't there to fix it. Only God and hard work could do that.

As we were leaving the lobby, we passed a bowl filled with scriptures with the sign "Pick up a blessing here". I pulled a paper out of the bowl and it read: Now the Lord is the Spirit, and where the Spirit of the Lord is, there is freedom. 2 Corinthians 3:17

"God is so good. This scripture is right on time. Hold onto it and read it when you feel weak," I said, putting the paper in her hand.

"Ok," she whispered and squeezed my arm even tighter.

We were led to her room at the very end of the first-floor hall on the right side. It was neat and clean with a simple queen-sized bed and night stand. The bedspread had a floral pattern with purple, pink and white flowers on it. Georgia wasn't a big fan of floral prints on bedding, but she would have to tolerate it this time. There was a lamp, alarm clock and Gideon bible on the night stand. Surprisingly, there were no refrigerators, microwaves or televisions in the rooms. All meals and snacks were served in the kitchen area and all TV was viewed in the common area.

While we were settling in, the lady in the room next to Georgia's knocked on the door and introduced herself. She appeared to be in her fifties and needed major dental work, but she had a beautiful spirit. She sat on the bed beside Georgia and grabbed both of her hands. I held my breath in anticipation of what she would say.

"My name is Mi Ling. You remind me of my first day here. My physical injuries were bad, but the ones to my heart were worse. You didn't do anything to deserve this. You are not the problem. Don't think God has forgotten about you. He will use this for His glory. He has great things planned for you. I can see it," she said softly.

"Thank you," Georgia said with a weak smile.

"I know you don't see it right now and what I'm saying is probably muddled with everything going on in your mind. No worries. It will come. I just felt led to share with you and deposit that seed." Mi Ling said, squeezed Georgia's hands and stood up.

When she walked passed me she gave me a knowing look and mouthed "Just be there" and went back into her room.

I looked at Georgia as she sat with her shoulders

hunched over and her head hanging low. I had never seen her so defeated. I felt helpless. Like Mi Ling said, I could only be there. Only the Lord could get her through this.

Chapter 12

Josiah was asleep when I got back to Mother Holmes' apartment. I was emotionally drained and wanted to get in my bed as soon as possible, but Mother Holmes asked me to stay for milk and cookies.

It felt good to rest myself in her cushioned chair after the night I had.

"How's your friend, baby?" she asked.

"She's going to be okay, but she has a long journey to take."

"What's going on with her?"

The story rushed out like I had been holding it deep in my soul for months and could finally set it free. I told her all about Georgia and Martin and the horrible things he had said and done. She closed her eyes and listened intently.

When I finished, she let out a huge sigh, opened her eyes and shook her head.

"Baby, she's going to end up right back with him before long. You need to bombard heaven for her."

"Why do you say that? I can't see her going back after everything that's happened. She seemed to feel safe at the shelter and the staff and residents are really supportive."

"He has a strong hold on her. It's very strong. She knows he's wrong, but she feels like he's the only choice she has. He's beaten her self-esteem and self-worth right out of her. Until she realizes who God says she is, she will stay. She was strong when you were with her, but alone she's weak. I know how she feels."

"How, Mother Holmes?"

"My first husband was abusive, but I stayed with him and endured it for years. It almost cost me my life. People don't like to talk about it, especially in the church. We act like we are immune, but we're not. My husband was a minister like your friend's husband. In fact, he was the pastor."

"What! Oh no, Mother Holmes! How awful! I can't believe a pastor would abuse his wife."

"Why not? He's a man ain't he? We put these ministers and pastors on pedestals and then we are shocked when they fall. Well, they shouldn't have been up there to begin with. That's why you must follow

Christ, not the pastor. They will disappoint you every time."

I usually didn't get into conversations with Mother Holmes about church. There was no doubt she was saved, but she rarely went to church. I could tell by some previous comments that she was dealing with some sort of church hurt, but I would never have imagined it was domestic violence. I had my own church hurt experience, but it was nothing compared to hers. If my husband/pastor abused me, I would stay away from church too.

"I don't think all ministers or pastors are bad Mother Holmes. The ones like Martin and your ex-husband give them a bad name. I try to judge each one individually."

"You're right. Not all of them are bad, but all the ones I've encountered are, so I just choose to stay away."

"Really, Mother Holmes? All of them," I laughed.

"Yes, all of them."

Her beautiful smile became a scowl and her entire body was rigid.

"Oh. Sorry. Tell me about it," I said, taken aback by her change in demeanor.

"It's getting late. You should get Josiah to bed. I will pray for your friend. Please keep me posted," she said, relaxing a little and standing up.

"Okay. Thanks for watching Josiah for me. I really appreciate it," I said, picking Josiah up from the couch and walking towards the door.

"You're welcome baby. See you later."

She opened the door for me and closed it quickly behind me. I guess I really struck a nerve. I hoped we would be able to share our experiences in more detail one day. I remembered mine like it was yesterday.

I attended my father's church when I first got saved, but soon realized it wasn't the place for me. A few months after Josiah was born, I decided to find a church that ministered to my needs at the time. I visited a few churches before I decided to join New Jerusalem. New Jerusalem was a progressive church filled with young people who were on fire for Jesus. The worship service was more like a praise party with praise dance, a full band and video presentations. I loved praise dance and wanted to join that ministry. I was told I had a natural rhythm and love for God that made me perfect for it.

Before I could join the praise dance ministry, I had to complete New Members Orientation, a six--week program that introduced new members to Christian living and the expectations of the church.

One of the church's seasoned members, Deacon Russell taught the classes. He had been a member for 20 years and a deacon for 10 of those years.

Deacon Russell was in his fifties, but looked like he was in his late thirties. He was very handsome with a bald head and a salt and pepper goatee. You could tell he was an athlete in his younger days and continued to work out. He was a widower of two years with two adult children. Rumors bounced off the walls of the church about him getting around with the ladies in the church. He supposedly had a special affection for the ladies in New Members Orientation. I figured the rumors were not true and were started by the other men who were jealous because a lot of the ladies swooned over him. I couldn't imagine a man of God would behave the way they described. I would soon find out the rumors were true, and I was his next mark.

He made his move after our final class celebration. He asked me to talk to him afterwards and I complied. I didn't understand that he wanted to do way more than talk.

He told me how proud he was of me and my progress in class. He said I was his star student and he saw a bright future for me at New Jerusalem. He reached over and touched my hand and foreboding feeling came over me. I pulled my hand away quickly.

"What's wrong baby? I've seen how you have been

looking at me. I know you want me to touch more than your hand," he said licking his lips.

I jumped up, knocked the chair over and backed away from him. As he walked towards me, his eyes scanned my body and I could see that he was aroused. I had never been so terrified in my life.

"Don't come near me! I have to leave!" I tried to yell, but my voice was caught in my throat and came out just above a whisper.

"You don't have to leave baby? I've noticed you in your tight dresses with all that booty and that nasty walk. I've wanted you from the moment I saw you. I know you want me too. You've been trying to get my attention by answering all the questions in class, laughing at my jokes and holding my hand extra-long when we shake hands. I've seen it all. Don't fight it baby," he said and grabbed my arm.

My voice broke free from the prison of my throat.

"Stop! Get your hands off me," I yelled as I pulled away from his grasp.

"Don't fight it baby. Don't fight it," he said, inching closer and closer to me.

I grabbed a pile of books off one of the tables and threw them at him as I made my escape. I ran full speed until I got into my car and drove off. That was the last time I set foot in New Jerusalem.

The experience left me disheartened about church. I thought it was a safe place from the wickedness of the world, but at that moment, it wasn't. It hurt that someone I trusted with my spiritual well-being would try to take advantage of me like that.

I didn't go to church for a few months, but I couldn't deny the yearning to go back. I needed more than I could get from "Bedside Baptist" service at home. I needed to fellowship with other believers. I needed the corporate worship experience and a right now word to get me through my week. I decided to search for a new church home, but I wasn't going to let myself be vulnerable to such an experience again.

When I found Faith Chapel, I felt like I had found my true home. Josiah enjoyed the children's ministry and they didn't have a New Members Orientation. That made it perfect. Although I had been at Faith Chapel for three years, I hadn't really delved into working in ministry. I attended worship service, Bible study and assisted with special events when asked, but I wasn't truly involved. I was still holding back because I didn't want to encounter another Deacon Russell. I would have loved to join the praise dance ministry at Faith Chapel, but I refused to do it. I was more like Mother Holmes than I wanted to admit. She stayed away from church because of her pain. I was there physically, but wasn't totally comfortable spiritually. I had to get over it, but the thought was too much for my brain to process at the time. I just needed to get some rest.

I put Josiah in bed and decided I would wash him up the next day. It would have been too much of a battle to wake him up and give him a bath. Just as I got him settled down my phone rang. Who in the world was calling me at 11 at night? I looked at the caller ID and it was Tony.

I hadn't been back to church since that Sunday Tony asked me out and I had the confrontation with Martin. I couldn't deal with the guilt and shame I felt when I was there. Tony and I exchanged text messages, but hadn't talked on the phone. He would send me a text every Sunday to let me know about the sermon and every Wednesday to let me know what they learned in Bible study. I would just respond back with "thanks". If he tried to start another conversation or asked to call I would cut things short. I knew I was being rude, but I really didn't want to talk to him. If I did, I might like him more and more only to be let down when he dropped me because of the baby. I couldn't go through that again, but this night I needed to hear his voice. Just as the call was about to go to voicemail, I picked up.

"Hello, may I speak to Maureen?" his beautiful voice asked.

"This is she," I said as sweetly as I could.

"I'm so sorry to call you this late, but I just felt like something was wrong, and I needed to call. A text message wouldn't work this time. The prompting was too much tonight. I hope you aren't angry," he said quickly, barely taking a breath.

"No. You're fine. It's nice to hear from you," I laughed.

"Oh good. How are you?" he asked, his voice filled with concern.

"I'm going to be okay. There has been a lot going on lately. I'm sure you have heard some things," I said hesitantly.

"I know you are pregnant if that's what you are talking about," he said quietly.

"Yes, it is. How do you feel about that?" I asked, holding my breath.

"It's definitely a shock. I just have one question."

"What is it?"

"Did you know when we went out?"

"Yes. I had just found out the week before," I said waiting for him to explode with anger and disgust. I wouldn't blame him.

"Okay. That explains why you were so shaken by your sister and cut our date short."

Was that all he was going to say? I thought he would be angry that I went out with him knowing I was carrying another man's baby.

"I don't blame you if you are angry with me and don't want anything else to do with me. I really like you and didn't think it was the right time to tell you," I rambled.

"I'm not angry Maureen, but I am disappointed. I really like you too, and I would hope you would have been upfront and honest with me. I don't like secrets."

"We were just getting to know each other. I didn't think I needed to reveal something so personal. I was trying to process it myself."

"I was trying to pursue a relationship with you and needed to know something that would affect our future like that."

"It was our first date. We didn't know what our future would be."

"You might not know, but I do. I told you the Lord showed you to me a long time ago. He told me you are my wife."

Was he serious? Was he crazy? Did the Lord really tell him that? Well, He hadn't told me anything. I was in no condition to be someone's wife right now. What was I supposed to say?

"Maureen, are you there?" he responded to my silence.

"Yes, I'm here."

"It's not every day that I tell someone they are my wife. I expected a different reaction," he laughed nervously.

"I don't know what to say. Are you sure it's me? I'm a mess right now. I just don't see how anyone would think I'm wife material."

"Yes, I'm sure. I guess I'm supposed to support you through the mess. God is going to make something beautiful out of it. I'm willing to step up and be there for you, Josiah and the new baby. Although they are not mine, I will love them like they are."

Those were words I dreamed of hearing a man say for so long. I wanted someone who would accept Josiah as their own and be there for us. Now a new baby was added to the mix, but this wonderful, handsome Godly man was saying he would be there despite that. He would love me and both of my children. It sounded too good to be true. Was this real or the enemy trying to trick me? I would really have to pray about this to be sure.

"This is overwhelming Tony. I need to pray about it

and see what the Lord says. You are such a wonderful man...."

"And you a wonderful woman."

"You are too kind."

"I'm just telling the truth. I will let you go. I know it's late. I will call you tomorrow to check on you. I promise it won't be so late. Are you sure you're okay?"

"Yes, I'm just tired. I will talk to you tomorrow. Have a great night."

"You too, sweetheart. Sweet dreams," he said and hung up.

I couldn't help but be excited about the possibility of being Mrs. Maureen Hudson. It would be a dream come true! I danced around the room to the music in my head, grabbed one of my plants and pretended like I was marching down the aisle to meet Tony at the end. I could see his handsome face smiling at me. I put the plant down and fell on the couch laughing.

What a day this had been. It started out with uncertainty and stress and ended with hope. That's how God works. I knew He would take care of me, the kids, Georgia, the other residents at Safe Haven, Monica, Tony and Mother Holmes. We were all in His hands. He was going to work it out. We just had to trust and believe.

Chapter 13

The next morning, I was awakened by Josiah shaking me. I looked at the clock and it was 8 am. Oh my God! I had overslept. I was late for work. I jumped up like something bit me.

"Mommy, get up. It's Saturday. You promised to take me to the park. I'm hungry. What's for breakfast? I want waffles," Josiah said excitedly.

"Slow down child. Let me get myself together. You can have waffles. Give me a minute and I will meet you in the kitchen." I said, getting up, holding my belly. It seemed like I got bigger overnight. According to Dr. Pearson, he or she was growing right on target and in a couple of months I was going to find out the sex. I'm not big on surprises so I needed to know what I was having so I could plan. I couldn't wait to find out!

"Wow, Mommy, the baby is getting big!" Josiah said,

reading my thoughts.

"You are so right, Josiah. Are you excited about being a big brother?"

"Yes ma'am! I get to tell the baby what to do and they must listen. That's going to be fun," he laughed.

"Like it's fun when Mommy tells you what to do?"

"Uh uh! Not like that Mommy. That's not fun at all," he said frowning.

I let out a hearty laugh and Josiah looked at me with disapproving eyes. I truly enjoyed being a mother. It was the best job I could ever have. I prayed daily that I would be able to teach him the right things and help him maneuver his way through life.

Being bi-racial put an added stress on his life. He had to balance both worlds and understand when people made fun of him or tried to make him choose. I knew all about the one drop rule that said one drop of Black blood makes you Black, but I didn't believe we needed to adhere to that. He wasn't just Black. He was both Black and White and he had to learn his own truth. People may have thought I was naïve for thinking that way, but I had to hold on to my convictions about the subject.

"Go on to the kitchen. I will be there in a minute."

"Okay Mommy," he said running out of my bedroom.

"Stop running," I yelled out behind him knowing it

was falling on deaf ears.

I called Georgia's boss the night before and told him she needed some time off. He was truly concerned about her wellbeing more than the job. I had never met him, but she always went on and on about Mr. Ross. At one point, I thought she had a thing for him, but she denied it. She said their relationship was totally professional and she didn't go for the swirl like me. I had to laugh because I didn't think I would ever go for it either until I met Roger.

While I was preparing waffles and bacon for Josiah I thought about the events of the day before. I was so glad Georgia was safe and away from Martin. I planned to ask Monica if she could watch Josiah for a little bit while I took some items to Georgia to make her stay more comfortable. I decided to call the shelter to check on her and confirm everything that she needed.

"Thank you for calling. How can I help you?" asked the receptionist.

"May I speak with Rachel? She's a new resident that came in last night," I asked.

For the sake of privacy, the residents all had code names. Georgia chose Rachel because she was her favorite Bible personality.

"Sure. One moment."

"Hello?" Georgia answered hesitantly.

"Hey girl. How are you?"

"I'm fine. When are you coming?"

"In a few. I wanted to go over your list one more time to make sure I have everything."

"Oh, I won't need for you to get the things on the list. I'm going home."

What? Had she lost her mind?

"You can't go home sweetie. You are safe where you are."

"I want to go home to my husband. I know he's sorry and he won't do it again. He loves me. I can't be here alone."

I could hear the tears in her voice and it broke my heart. I let out a deep breath so that I could keep my composure. I knew she was vulnerable and I didn't want to say the wrong thing.

"You need to stay where you are, Georgia. He can't hurt you there. Going back isn't good for either of you."

"I don't care about that. I want to leave! Come get me now!" she said through gritted teeth.

I wouldn't be her friend if I allowed her to go back to that situation. She might have been mad at me forever, but I couldn't do it.

"Okay. I will be there shortly," I said softly.

Arguing with her wasn't going to help so I relented. I would have to wait to talk to her in person to change her mind.

"Thank you so much. I don't mean to be demanding, but I can't spend another minute here. Please get here as quick as you can."

We said our goodbyes and ended the call. I prayed for the right words to say to reassure her that everything would be alright.

Chapter 14

When I arrived, the receptionist was frazzled and nervous. I saw several staff members scurrying around. The atmosphere was not calm and peaceful like the day before. I approached the front desk cautiously.

"Hello. My name is Maureen Mason. I'm here to see Rachel."

"Oh, thank God! Please come this way!" she exclaimed and jumped out of her seat.

What in the world was going on? I noticed as I followed her that we were headed to Georgia's room. That's also where the staff was going. Residents peered out of their doors with concern. I saw Mi Ling pacing down the hall with her head bowed. It appeared she was praying.

The closer we got to her room, the louder I could hear Georgia screaming. I couldn't make out what she was saying, but the sound was gut-wrenching.

Georgia was standing on top of her bed. She had taken all the covers off the bed and was on the bare mattress. The nightstand was knocked over and there were papers all over the floor. Her eyes were darting around the room and her face was contorted. The closer the staff got to her, the louder she screamed. She wasn't Georgia. It was like something demonic had overtaken her. I was afraid, but I knew I was the only one that might be able to calm her down.

The receptionist whispered to one of the staff members and pointed at me. They motioned for me to come closer.

"She's been like this for the past 20 minutes. It happened suddenly. We announced that it was time for Zumba class and asked if she wanted to join us and she flipped out. It was like she became a different person. I don't understand what set her off, but we can't seem to calm her. We were preparing to call the crisis unit, but maybe you can get her to calm down, so we can talk to her and find out what the trigger was," said a middle-aged woman with dark brown hair pulled back into a bun. Her name tag read Dr. Sandra Stevenson, PhD.

"I will try," I said and walked into the room.

Immediately, when Georgia saw me her demeanor changed. The wild look left her eyes and she smiled. She jumped off the bed, ran to me and gave me a big hug.

"Thank God you're here to take me away from this place! I can't take it here."

"Georgia, sweetheart, what's going on?"

"What do you mean?"

"Look around honey. Look at what you did," I said and motioned around the room.

A look of shock covered her face. It was as if she didn't remember anything that just happened. She didn't know how the room was destroyed.

"I did this?" she asked.

"Yes sweetie. Do you know why? What were you upset about?"

"I don't know…"

"They said they asked you if you wanted to go to Zumba and you flipped out."

The wild look began to rear its ugly head and she balled up her fist.

"I don't need to go to Zumba! I'm not fat! He said I was fat, but I'm not!" she yelled.

"No, you're not fat. It's okay. It's okay," I said as I hugged her tightly.

Her body went limp in my arms and her sobs quieted as I rocked her. I looked at Dr. Stevenson and she smiled gently as she approached us.

"You don't have to do anything you don't want to do Rachel. Let's go have a talk," Dr. Stevenson said softly.

"I don't want to talk to you," Georgia said like a defiant child.

"I will go with you. I think you need to talk with Dr. Stevenson. She can help," I said.

"No, she can't. I want to get out of here," Georgia said, pushing away from me.

"You can't leave just yet. Let's talk to Dr. Stevenson and then see how you feel. Trust me. You trust me, right?" I asked.

"Yes, Maureen. I trust you with my life," she said with such intensity it scared me. It was at that moment that I realized the responsibility I had taken on with this situation.

"Okay. Let's go to my office and chat ladies," Dr. Stevenson said, walking away slowly, waiting for us to follow.

I gently tugged Georgia and she moved with me. I knew this was going to be a challenge because Georgia didn't trust "head doctors" as she called them.

As we walked away, the staff began to straighten up Georgia's room and the residents went back into their rooms. Mi Ling was still praying as we passed.

Dr. Stevenson's office was comfortable and calming.

The walls were painted light blue and she had pictures of beach scenes on the walls. It reminded me of my bedroom; calming and relaxing. There was a couch with a dark blue slipcover and blue and green pillows on it and two oak chairs with blue cushions positioned in front of the desk. She motioned for us to sit in the chairs and she sat behind her desk.

"Well, Rachel we've had quite an eventful morning, haven't we?" Dr. Stevenson asked smiling.

"I guess so." Georgia replied.

"I understand it was the request for you to participate in the Zumba class that triggered you. Tell me about your feelings about exercise and weight?"

"Look lady, I'm not here for you to psycho analyze me and make me feel crazy. I don't need a head doctor to tell me I have issues. We all have issues," Georgia spat.

"Georgia, please behave!" I interjected.

"It's okay. She has a right to her feelings. I'm not here to make you feel crazy Rachel. I'm here to help you work through your feelings and the trauma that you have been through. Being in an abusive relationship does a number on your self-esteem. It takes work to build it back up. You have to be willing to do the work."

"What do you know about it? You know nothing about my life and how to help me. You just have your books and the psycho-babble they taught you. How is that going to help me?" Georgia exclaimed, getting up out of her chair and glaring at Dr. Stevenson.

Dr. Stevenson was taken aback by Georgia's hostility and I saw the nervousness in her face. I knew she was thankful I was there. Despite her nerves, she remained calm.

"I do know Rachel. I don't know exactly how you feel in your exact circumstances, but I know what it's like to be abused. I went through 10 years of abuse with my first husband. It was what drove me to want to complete my doctorate, so I could be a source of comfort for women like myself. I want to know you, so I can help you. Our residents leave here stronger and healthier mentally, physically and emotionally and strive for great things in their lives. I know you can be one of those success stories as well, but I need for you to trust me."

"Oh. I'm sorry for my outburst Dr. Stevenson. I'm sorry for what you went through. Sometimes it feels like I'm all alone and no one understands," Georgia said and sat back down.

"That's okay. I know about being angry at the world and feeling like no one could ever understand or help. I want to help you. I know God will show me the way and we will work through it together."

"I don't know. It seems God has forgotten about me," Georgia said with tears in her eyes.

"Oh no! He hasn't forgotten about you. He will never leave or forsake you."

I needed that reminder as well. I felt that God had forgotten about me, but He had shown me recently that He was still there. He turned things around with my relationship with Monica. He may have brought my husband into my life, but the jury was still out on that. He led us to the right place for Georgia. I believed Safe Haven was the blessing she needed. He was truly our help in times of trouble.

"I guess so," Georgia said quietly.

"Let's schedule some more sessions so we can get to know each other and develop a plan for you Rachel. I'm here Monday through Thursday, eight to five and Friday, eight - noon. What days next week work for you? I think we should start out with twice a week and then see how things go from there. I will also give you my contact information in case you need to chat outside of our appointment times."

"Mondays and Wednesdays, I guess. How long do you think I will have to stay here?"

"The average resident stays three to six months. Some stay shorter times and still see me for appointments on an outpatient basis. I meet those clients outside of the facility."

"That's a long time. I don't know..."

"We will just take it one week at a time. I will see you Mondays and Wednesdays at 1pm. How does that sound?" Dr. Stevenson asked.

"That's good. I will see you then," Georgia said standing up.

The women shook hands. I shook hands with Dr. Stevenson and walked out with Georgia.

"She's crazy if she thinks I'm staying here for three to six months," Georgia said angrily.

"It may not take that long. Don't focus on that. Just focus on getting help and ridding yourself of Martin and his abusive ways. You are so much better than that."

"It's not that easy, Maureen. He's my husband, but you wouldn't know about that since you don't have one," she sneered.

I let that comment pass because she was a ball of emotions and I didn't want to set her off again. Normally it would have upset me, but husband or not, I had bigger fish to fry. I had to get through this pregnancy.

"I know it's not easy. I'm here to help however I can. Speaking of that, here are your supplies. If you need for me to get something else I will," I said, giving her the tote bag on my shoulder. I didn't realize I was still carrying it with everything going on.

"That's fine. Thanks," she said, taking the bag.

"Promise me you will behave until I come back and check on you. I will call you later today,"

"I promise. I'm good. Thank you for everything," she said and gave me a quick hug.

I hugged her back and walked her to her room. The staff had put everything back in order and her room was neat again. She went in and sat on her bed.

"Take care lovely," I said and waved goodbye.

"Bye," she said and laid down on the bed. I knew she would be asleep shortly. I closed her door behind me.

Mi Ling peeked out of her room door and gave me a thumb up. I knew she would watch out for Georgia for me. I waved goodbye to her and left.

I felt good about Georgia and Dr. Stevenson, but I was still a little nervous about Georgia's mood swings. I would have to check on her often to make sure she was doing what she was supposed to do. It was like having another child. Just then, I felt a flutter in my belly and smiled.

"I can't wait to meet you little one. You're going to be the peace my crazy world needs."

Chapter 15

"It's a girl!" Dr. Pearson announced.

I was laying on the bed in the examination room with my eyes covered anticipating the news. I was excited to have a mini-me to raise. Visions of pink dresses, hair bows, and Barbie dolls danced in my head.

"Really!" I said, sitting up a little to view the ultrasound monitor.

"Yes. You can see right there," Dr. Pearson said, pointing at my little girl's private parts on the screen. "It's definitely a girl."

"Yay! I'm so excited. I can't wait to tell Josiah and Monica."

Things had been on the upswing for the past couple of months. I had moments of doubt and worry, but I pushed through them.

I continued to work through my feelings about that

night with Roger and what it meant for me spiritually. I knew I was forgiven, but sometimes I didn't believe I deserved it. I worried about what people thought about me, my relationship with God and my children. I made some unholy decisions, but things in my life were falling into place. The Bible says, everything works together for the good of those who love the Lord and are called according to His purpose. I loved Him with my heart, soul and mind and despite my faults, He had a purpose for me.

My relationship with Monica was amazing. We talked every day about the baby, work and, Lord forgive us, the neighborhood gossip. We were getting along better than we had our entire lives.

Georgia was doing well at Safe Haven. Working with Dr. Stevenson was just what she needed. She accepted the three to six-month stay and even said she would miss it once she graduated. She applied for FMLA and was blessed that her job would be waiting for her when she returned to the real world.

Roger sent a couple more letters and called, but I didn't bother opening the letters or answering the calls. I was done with him and whatever he had to say.

I was scared out of my mind the first Sunday I went back to church. I felt like everyone was judging me until one of the church mothers searched for me and gave me a big hug. She told me she loved me, and God did too. I needed to hear those words more than anything. After that, I could relax and enjoy the service.

Tony was glad I was back in church and we were getting to know each other better. We even went back to Hannah's for a redo first date. I wasn't sure if he was my husband, but I enjoyed his company.

Martin stopped attending Faith Chapel after Georgia went to Safe Haven and I was so thankful for that. From what I heard, the congregation at Grace and Deliverance was bamboozled and had no clue how evil and abusive he was. He told them Georgia was traveling a lot with her job and would miss several Sundays. I wondered how long he could keep up that lie, but that wasn't my problem. If Georgia was good, I was good.

"I know they will be thrilled. Josiah is going to be such a great big brother. He's so sweet," Dr. Pearson said as she wiped the gel off my belly.

"Yes, he is. I love him so much. I worry I may not have enough love for him and his sister."

"No worries about that. Just like God has enough love to go around to everyone in the world, he gifted mothers with the ability to love multiple children. It's going to be a blessing."

"You are so right, Dr. Pearson."

"I usually am."

We looked at each other and laughed so loud one of the nurses peeked in on us.

"What's so funny?" she prodded.

"Oh, nothing. It's an insider. You wouldn't understand," Dr. Pearson said, waving her away.

The nurse smiled and closed the door. I was so glad I was Dr. Pearson's patient. She and her staff were professional, friendly and supportive.

"Thank you so much for being such a great mentor and doctor for me Dr. Pearson. I don't tell you often, but I really appreciate you," I said, getting up and giving her a quick hug.

"You're most welcome Maureen. It's been a pleasure. Things are going well with your little lady. I will see you at your next appointment."

"See you then." I said as she walked out the door.

I couldn't wait to call Monica and tell her about the baby.

"It's a girl!" I yelled into the phone.

"I told you! I'm going to have a niece! I'm going to have a niece!"

"You're so silly. I think you're happier than I am."

"I'm happy we're learning how to be true sisters. It's

like we've been given another chance. I'm here to support you all the way. I know you didn't want to have another baby like this, but I know the Lord is going to work it out."

"What? Listen to you sounding all deep and spiritual. What's gotten into you?" I laughed.

"Nothing. Just counting my blessings today. It has me feeling warm and fuzzy. You better enjoy it while it lasts."

"You're too much! How about we meet at Sam's Deli for lunch tomorrow? I know how much you like their salads. I'm feeling good so it's my treat."

"Wow! You're feeling very good. You need to get pregnant more often," she laughed.

It felt so good to have an enjoyable conversation with my sister. Our parents would have been so proud.

Next, it was time to tell Josiah. I wanted to make the big reveal extra special so I decided to run into Crossroads Market and buy a pink "I love my big brother" bib to help me make the announcement. I couldn't wait to see the look on his face.

I was looking at the bibs when I heard footsteps approach and stop close behind me. I felt hot breath on my neck. I jumped and turned around quickly.

"Where's my wife?" Martin growled at me.

"None of your business. If you treated her right, she would be with you," I snapped.

I was trying to act like he didn't bother me, but I was scared. His eyes were wide, and he was flexing his fingers preparing to close them into a fist. I didn't think he was crazy enough to hit a pregnant woman in a public place, but maybe he was.

"Don't get smart with me Maureen. She's my wife and I need to know where she is. My ordination and initial sermon are coming up this weekend. She has to be there."

I couldn't believe what I was hearing. He didn't care about her well-being or anything other than having her at his ordination as some trophy wife or something.

"Well, I doubt she will be at your sad excuse of an ordination. You shouldn't be a minister much less an Assistant Pastor. May God have mercy on your soul!"

"Don't you dare cast judgment on me! You're pregnant out of wedlock, not once, but twice. Your man is in jail, but you are trying to move on quickly with someone else. You're just a whore and a Jezebel pretending to be holy. Don't you say anything about me, little girl!" he said stepping closer to me.

I searched the aisle, but no one was around. There was no one there to protect me, but I made the choice to stand up for myself and Georgia in that moment. I couldn't be quiet and run away. He had no right to bully me. I couldn't physically fight him because I was pregnant, but I could fight with my words. I was going to tell the truth and shame the devil.

"I may have children out of wedlock, but at least don't beat women to make me feel better about myself. A real man doesn't put his hands on a woman. A real man can handle the truth and doesn't blame others for his mistakes. A real man takes care of his woman and makes her feel loved. He doesn't beat her self-esteem away and make her feel less than her worth. You're not a man! You're not a minister or assistant pastor. You are the devil!"

His lips spread into a grin that rivaled that of the Joker from Batman and his laughter was loud and unexpected.

"I'm the devil, huh? You are ridiculous! I'm not going to entertain this conversation anymore. Tell me where my wife is so I can leave."

"I'm not telling you anything...."

Before I could finish my statement, he grabbed my arm and pulled me close to him. It was like Deacon Russell all over again. Here was another so called Godly man who thought he could take advantage of me. I didn't know what to do. If I screamed, he might hurt me for real. If I pulled away, I might fall. I closed my eyes and willed for him to let me go.

"Listen, little girl. I'm not playing games with you. Georgia better be at my ordination if you know what's good for you. If she's not, you will regret it," he said and let go of my arm.

I was in shock. My heart was pounding out of my chest and I felt weak. My feet were stuck, and I couldn't move. My voice was locked in my throat and I couldn't speak. My eyes were closed tightly, and tears poured down my face.

"Are you okay ma'am?" asked a young voice.

I opened my eyes and saw her face covered in too much makeup and concern. She had piercing blue eyes and black hair cut into a bob. Short shorts and a crop top covered her slim frame.

"Yes, I'm okay. Thank you," I said, wiping away the tears. I looked around for Martin. He was nowhere to be found. He disappeared as quickly as he appeared.

"Are you sure? You're shaking."

"I just got into an argument with someone. I just need to go home and calm down. Thank you for your concern," I said. My feet became unstuck and I started to walk away.

"Were you talking to Mr. Martin Long?" she asked.

How did she know Martin? I stopped walking and turned towards her.

"Yes."

"Did he say something to upset you? He's a horrible man. Just horrible," she said with a far-a-way look in her eyes. It was like a bad memory had invaded her mind.

"How do you know Mr. Long?"

"I go to college with his daughter, Tyra. We are best friends,"

Did she just say Tyra? Was it the same "Tyra" Georgia and Martin were fighting about?

"I didn't know Martin had a daughter."

"I'm not surprised. He has denied her existence all her life. He gave her mother money and that's all. He's never spent any time with Tyra nor celebrated one birthday. Her mom died last year, and she reached out to him. He got mad because she called his house. He told her not to contact him ever again. He said he fulfilled his promise to her mother and now that she was gone that was it. Tyra was devastated!"

Martin had some skeletons in his closet, but had nerve enough to talk about me. I couldn't believe he would deny his own flesh and blood like that. Georgia delayed her dream of having children for him. He said he didn't want children to interrupt his goals in ministry. He said they could have children once he was established in his own church, but the whole time he already had a child.

"Wow! I had no idea. I'm sorry, but what's your name?"

"Kristen. Kristen Brown," she said and held out her hand for me to shake.

"My name is Maureen Mason. It's nice to meet you Kristen," I said, accepting her hand.

"When I saw him grab you and then rush away, I had to stop and do something. I could tell he was up to no good. I don't know what your argument was about, but you should be careful."

"I will. I have had problems with him before and he has hurt someone I love."

"He's a monster."

"Kristen, I would like to speak to Tyra. Do you think she would talk to me? Martin's wife is my best friend. Maybe we can figure out how to get him to take responsibility for his actions."

"I can talk to her about it. Dealing with Mr. Long can be risky. Put your number in my phone," she said, handing me her cell phone.

I saved my number on her phone and she promised

to give it to Tyra when she saw her later that evening. She called my phone, so I could save her number as well. I knew speaking to Tyra would be the key to bringing Martin down a peg or two.

Kristen and I said goodbye, I grabbed a bib and went to the checkout line. I couldn't help but look around to make sure Martin wasn't following me. I looked over my shoulder as I walked to my car. I even looked in the back seat before getting in. I knew the Lord didn't give us the spirit of fear, but Martin had done a number on me. I couldn't let it overwhelm me. I wasn't going to live in fear of no man, especially not Martin.

I turned on the radio and "The Battle is Not Yours" by Yolanda Adams was playing. Was that a sign that I needed to back off and let the Lord fight the battle with Martin? If it was, it was a sign that I ignored. Before my thoughts were, if Georgia was good, I was good, but he made it personal. He threatened to hurt me and that was taking it too far. This was my battle and I was going to win.

Chapter 16

My mood changed from worry to excitement when I pulled up to the daycare. I wanted to focus on the good news I was going to share with Josiah, not my encounter with Martin.

"Hi Mama!" Mrs. Calhoun exclaimed when she saw me signing Josiah out. "How are you?"

"I'm great Mrs. Calhoun. How are you?"

"I'm well. Josiah had a great day. He's so smart!"

"Of course, he is. Look at who his mom is," I laughed.

"You're right. You're right," she replied nodding.

"I have some exciting news to tell him today. That's why I'm picking him up early."

"Oh really. Do tell."

I pulled the bib out of my purse and handed it to her.

"Oh Mama! This is wonderful!"

"Shhh! Let's keep this hush until I tell Josiah. Then

you can let the world know tomorrow," I said, stuffing the bib back in my purse.

"You know I will," she beamed. "Josiah Mason, prepare to leave," she said into her walkie talkie.

Moments later Josiah came running around the corner screaming, "I'm ready to go Mommy!"

"You can't go without your bookbag, son. You're always forgetting that bookbag," I laughed.

Josiah went back to the classroom to find his bookbag. Mrs. Calhoun grabbed my hand and turned me towards her.

"I'm so proud of you Mama," she said, her tone serious, but filled with love.

"Really? I don't know if my situation is anything to be proud of."

"No ma'am. Hold your head up. I'm proud of you because you haven't let this shake your faith and break you down. I can see in your face that it's difficult, but you are pressing on. Don't let anyone make you feel less than the woman of God that you are. That is unacceptable."

Her words washed over me like a waterfall. She said exactly what I needed to hear at that moment. That evening with Roger and everything after made me question my salvation. I knew my love for God was real, but was that enough? Her words gave me a boost of confidence.

"I'm ready now, Mommy," Josiah said coming back around the corner with his book bag on his back.

"Great. Let's go. How about we go to Chick in a Bun?"

"Yay! You're the best Mommy ever!"

We all laughed, and I gave Mrs. Calhoun a quick hug before we left. She smiled at me and her smile was warm and genuine. It made me feel like everything was going to be alright.

Josiah filled me in on his day. He had sausage and waffles for breakfast. After breakfast, they had center time and he played construction with his friends Emery and Donovan. After center time, they worked on their ABCs and sight words. He was the only one who knew all the sight words and he was extremely proud of that. They had spaghetti, green beans, applesauce and a roll for lunch. He didn't eat the green beans because they were yucky. Next, they laid down for their naps. After naptime, they had a snack and then it was story time. I got there during story time. They were going to have water play after story time. He was upset he was going to miss it, but he would rather be with me. At least that's how I understood it all. The ramblings of a four -year- old can get lost in translation if you don't listen attentively.

I was listening, but my mind kept wandering to what

Mrs. Calhoun said. "Don't let anyone make you feel less than the woman of God that you are". What a powerful statement. I decided at that moment that I would no longer let other people's perceptions of me shape my perception of myself. I was a woman of God despite my mistakes and lapses in judgment. It didn't make me perfect, but it made me redeemed. I said those words to others when I defended myself and my faith, but I didn't truly believe them until that moment. I felt free.

"Mommy we're here! Let's go in!" Josiah yelled about to jump out of his booster seat with excitement.

I was so deep in thought I didn't realize we had arrived and pulled into a parking space. Thank God, for traveling mercies.

We were greeted by the smell of fresh French fries, the sound of drinks pouring from the drink machine, smiling faces and laughter. I loved Chick in a Bun. Their chicken sandwiches and fries were the best in town.

When I walked up to the counter I was surprised to see Kristen standing there. She was no longer in her crop top and shorts, but wore the same white shirt and black pants as the other workers. She had removed some of her make up for a more polished look.

"May I take your order?" she asked like we didn't meet an hour ago. I took her lead and did the same.

"Yes. Can we have a nugget kid's meal with an apple juice and a number one with lemonade to drink?"

"What kind of sauce for your nuggets?"

"No sauce please!" Josiah interrupted.

"Okay little man. No sauce," she laughed. "You are so cute! How old are you?"

"I'm four. How old are you?"

"Josiah! You don't ask a lady her age!" I exclaimed.

"It's okay. I'm 18, sweetie."

"Is this for here or to go?" she asked, turning her attention back to me.

"Here," I responded.

She finished ringing up our order and I paid her. We found a seat and waited for the food to be delivered. Josiah ate way too fast because he was ready to play. I tried to remind him to slow down a couple of times, but it was no use. Once he was finished he jumped up and ran to take his shoes off.

Whenever we came to the play area, he had so much fun he would wear himself out. I loved watching him and the other children. Sometimes I would strike up a conversation with one of the other parents, but I wasn't in the mood that day. I just wanted to sit quietly and reflect on the day's events.

My thoughts were interrupted by a tall young lady

with a large bosom and jet black curly shoulder-length hair.

"Hi ma'am. I'm so sorry to bother you, but are you Maureen Mason?" she asked quietly.

"Yes, I am. And you are?" I asked, although I already knew who she was. She had her father's eyes.

"I'm Tyra Campbell. You met my friend Kristen earlier today. She told me about you when we got to work today. She said your son is adorable. Which one is he?" she asked, searching the play area.

"The one right there coming out of the red slide," I said pointing to Josiah.

"He's such a cutie!" she exclaimed, her voice going up an octave.

"Thank you so much. Yes, I met Kristen at Crossroads Market earlier today. She told me a little about you and your father's relationship or lack of one. He's married to my best friend."

"You're friends with Mrs. Georgia? She was so nice to me when my mom died. Kristen said you wanted to talk to me about making him take responsibility for his actions. I'm not sure what I can do. He doesn't want anything to do with me," she said, her voice dropping down to just above a whisper.

"I'm so sorry to hear that Tyra. Have a seat and let's

chat," I said, motioning her to sit down.

"Oh no. I can't talk long. I took a quick break and I have to get back to work soon."

"Oh, I see. Well, like I told Kristen I didn't even know Martin had a child and I've known him for three years. He's being ordained and doing his initial sermon this weekend, but he has no business being a minister."

"You're right about that," she said, wrinkling her face.

"I want to confront him with his skeletons and make him see the error of his ways. He can't be a wolf in sheep's clothing leading the people of God astray. I can't stand for it!" I yelled, banging my fist on the table.

Several parents looked our way. I mouthed "Sorry" and they went back to attending to their children.

"I'm not sure I want to get involved with that. You're so intense. Do you have a plan?" Tyra asked.

"Not exactly." I responded.

"I need to think about this. I must figure out how my mother would want me to handle things."

"I'm so sorry about your mother. I lost mine when I was twelve, so I can relate to how you feel."

"Thank you. It's the hardest thing I've ever been through. She was my best friend," she said as a single tear escaped her eyelids and slid down the side of her cheek. I handed her a napkin.

"Yes, yes. It's very hard," I said, blinking away tears.

"How's Mrs. Georgia?" she asked, wiping her face.

"Your father beat her up pretty bad, but she's somewhere safe now. She's working to heal."

"Oh, no! Please tell her I said hi and I hope she's better soon. I hate to cut this short, but my break is over. I will call you later tonight. I promise," she said and hurried away.

I felt a connection with Tyra. It went beyond losing our mothers at a young age. I could tell she had seen and been through a lot in her young life. She was a survivor and so was I. Her quiet demeanor didn't fool me. There was something brewing deep within and you wouldn't want to be around when it came bubbling up.

I began the process of reeling Josiah in so we could go. I would have to call him five or six times to get him to stop playing and another three or four to get him to put his shoes back on.

He fell asleep quickly during the drive home. I looked back at him in the rear-view mirror and before I knew it tears were rolling down my face. They were tears of uncertainty. What was the future going to hold for him? He would be a teenager by the time his father got out of jail. I didn't want him to be a statistic because his father wasn't present. The streets were not going to claim my precious son! He was going to grow up in the love of the Lord and he was going to make something of himself. I was going to see to that.

When I got home and checked the mail, I discovered another letter from Roger. Just when I was thinking about what it would be like if Josiah didn't have his father in his life, his father reached out. "I hear you Lord," I said aloud. Everything in me wanted to throw it in the trash, but I needed to hear him out. I couldn't cut him out of our life. He was my children's father and I had to face what that meant. I decided to read the letter after Josiah went to bed.

After his bedtime routine, I told Josiah I had a surprise for him.

"What is it Mommy? A new toy!" he said with excitement.

"No, not a new toy,"

"A bike? A phone? What Mommy?"

"Boy, you know you are too young for a phone," I laughed. "I found out if you are going to have a baby brother or a baby sister."

"Yay! I hope it's a brother,"

"Close your eyes."

He closed his eyes and I put the bib in his hand.

"Open your eyes."

He looked at the bib for a moment and then threw it down.

"I don't want no sister!" he cried.

I didn't expect that reaction. I had never seen him so upset.

"Why not, Josiah?"

"I don't want no sister 'cause I can't help her if she gets in trouble."

"What do you mean?"

"I can't help Auntie Georgia when Uncle Martin hurts her. I can't help you when you are sad. Pastor Green said men are supposed to be nice and help women, but I can't."

I grabbed him and held him tight. I had no idea he was so sensitive to everything going on with me and Georgia. I hate he witnessed the altercation between Martin and Georgia. I tried to hide it when I was troubled or sad. I guess I didn't do as good of a job as I thought. I had to fight back the tears, so I wouldn't make him even more upset.

I wasn't sure what to say to give him peace. The Lord had to give me the words. I pulled him away from me and looked in his eyes.

"It isn't your job to help me and Auntie Georgia, honey. Your job is to love us. Your hugs and kisses make us feel better. You don't have to worry about adult problems. God will help us. You will be a great big brother. Your sister will look up to you and you can show her the right way to do things and how to love God. You are not a man, yet so you don't have to worry about all of that. Just continue to be the sweet little boy that you are."

"Are you sure Mommy?"

"Yes, I'm sure sweetheart. You don't need to worry. We're going to be fine."

"Can I give you hugs whenever you are sad?"

"You sure can. I would love that."

He wrapped his arms as far as they would go around my belly and squeezed tight.

"That's for you and Heaven"

"Who's Heaven?"

"The baby," he laughed.

"Why do you call her Heaven?"

"Because God made heaven and He made her."

"Okay. Sounds good. Now let's go to sleep. Say your prayers."

He said his prayers and included Heaven in his list of those God should bless.

Heaven Mason. It had a nice ring to it. Josiah was so right. God made her, and I believed she would be a piece of heaven here on Earth for us. The thought gave me peace. It was like the Holy Spirit rested on me and let me know I was carrying a blessing. I felt like how Mary, the mother of Jesus, must have felt when she realized the gift she was carrying. Heaven wasn't conceived in the way I would have liked, but she was destined for greatness. She was going to change our world for the good.

I took an extra-long bath, relaxed my nerves and listened to nothing but my thoughts. Having quiet time to reflect was wonderful. I was sure Roger's letter was going to make me mad, so I had to get my mind right before I read it.

Dear Maureen,

You didn't write back, and you won't accept my calls. I know you're angry with me about my confession. I deserve it, but I don't regret telling you. Confession is good for the soul even when you must face the consequences.

We talked about confession in Bible study last week. Confession is the first step to salvation, but it continues after that. They taught us that you must confess and repent daily, not just to God, but others. I have made confessions to my mom and friends too. I had to do it to clear my heart. If you stay mad at me forever and never come see me, I still know I did the right thing. I hope that's not the case. I'm learning and growing Maureen. I'm really trying to be better for you and our children. I love you. You may not believe it, but I do.

Please forgive me. Don't forgive me for me, but for you. Don't let being angry at me block your blessings. We learned about that in Bible study too.

Please come see me so we can talk things out in person. I would love to see the ultrasound pics or something. Do you know if it's a girl or a boy yet? I don't like to beg, but please come.

I have enclosed the application again. Sunday is the next visitation day. You can bring the application with you instead of mailing it back to me since it's so soon.

I've sent a picture and a note for Josiah. Please give it to him when the time is right. Again, I love you.

Yours always,
Roger

I pulled out a wonderful picture of Mickey Mouse wearing a baseball uniform. It was addressed "To Daddy's little slugger, Josiah". Roger always talked about

Josiah being a Major League Baseball star one day. The note at the bottom of the picture read "We may be apart, but we are in each other's hearts. Never forget that. I love you. Daddy"

I read the letter and note to Josiah at least five times before I put it back in the envelope. Tears covered my face as I put the envelope inside my Bible and placed the Bible on my nightstand. He was so right. Confession was good for the soul and forgiveness were necessary. I had to forgive him, but did that mean we were supposed to be together? Was Tony the man for me? Tony said I was his wife. Roger said he loves me, but his actions haven't always showed it. He was changing, but was it too little, too late. Did I still love him? I wasn't sure, but I decided I would go see him. I needed to judge for myself if he was being sincere. Sunday was Martin's ordination day, so I would have to visit the next time.

My mind was all over the place as I tried to fall asleep. The events of the day played over and over like a soap opera. I had experienced all the excitement, anger, fear, joy and intrigue I could handle for one day.

I prayed for relief and focused on Heaven. What would she look like? Whose personality would she have? None of that really mattered. She was mine and I loved her more than life already.

Chapter 17

Tyra called and woke me up around 10 pm. She apologized for calling so late, but I really didn't mind. I was anxious to devise our "Martin Smackdown".

"I used to cry myself to sleep at night wondering why my Daddy didn't love me. I wanted a relationship with him so bad, but he didn't care. Mommy would try to make excuses for him, but I saw right through them," she said softly. I could feel the pain behind every word and my heart went out to her.

"What kinds of excuses?" I asked.

"She said they were both young and it was his parents that made the decisions. She was 13 and he was 14 so I understood why they didn't have control over things in the beginning. Her parents went along with things because his father was chairman of the deacons and his mother was head of the missionaries, whatever that was supposed to mean. I never understood all the church the church politics. It seems like someone's position is more important than doing the right thing. Mommy said they were grooming him to be a minister and didn't want anything to stop him from reaching that goal. I would think he would have realized that what they were doing was wrong. He should have reached out to us to make things right, but he was more worried about his image. That's why I don't go to church now. It's filled with fake people who are in love with themselves more than God. They say they love Jesus, but they sure don't act like it," she said raising her voice.

"Yes, you would think he would have done the right thing, but not all church people are like that. I go to church and I'm not fake."

"Not being rude, Ms. Maureen, but I don't know you like that. I will have to see that for myself."

Wow! I was shocked she spoke to me that way, but I appreciated her honesty and boldness.

"I wish I didn't hate him, but I do," she continued.

"Hate is a strong word, Tyra. You don't want to have hate in your heart, but I understand you not liking him because of his lack of attention to you and your mother."

I didn't want her to harbor hate and ill will in her heart towards her father or anyone for that matter. Hate was a prison that kept my heart hostage for years after Roger and I broke up. It was a very painful part of my life. Once I let it go I had such peace. I wanted her to have the same peace; peace beyond her understanding. The peace that only God can give.

"I understand what you are saying Ms. Maureen, but I can't help how I feel right now. I hate him and I'm willing to do whatever you have planned to show him just that. I'm so upset to hear he hurt Mrs. Georgia. She is so sweet."

I was glad we were of one accord. We talked for another 30 minutes and put our heads together to devise our plan. We decided we needed to let Georgia know about it. I told Tyra I would visit her the next day.

A few moments after I hung up with Tyra, my phone rang again. It was Tony. I really cared about Tony, but I had to admit I still had feelings for Roger. He apologized and seemed sincere. I didn't know what that meant for us. I was so confused.

"Hey sweetheart. How are you beautiful?" he asked with his sexy baritone voice.

"I'm doing okay. I have a lot going on right now."

"What's wrong? Can I help?" he asked, his voice filled with worry.

I told him about my confrontation with Martin,

meeting Kristen and my conversation with Tyra moments prior. Retelling it was almost as exhausting as going through it.

"He did what? He better be glad I'm saved. The old me would bust a cap in his behind for that. No one should handle a woman like that, especially a pregnant one. Are you sure you're okay?" he asked.

"Yes, I'm fine. He shook me up, but physically I'm good. Georgia has been through far worse with him. He needs to pay. He can't bully women anymore and get away with it. Denying his own flesh and blood is the worst type of bullying. She's such a sweet girl. It's a shame she's hurting so much."

"He's a sorry excuse of a man. Who treats women the way he does and then declares they are called to minister to God's people? It's not right."

"Exactly! That's why our plan must work. He can't be ordained and lead people astray."

"I know you're upset and I am too, but I don't think you need to do anything. Let the Lord handle him. His wrath is worse than anything you could dish out."

"Martin isn't a true man of God and I wouldn't be a true woman of God if I stood by and did nothing about him being a false prophet."

"I don't know about that Maureen. I don't think you

should get involved."

"Well, I disagree. If you have a problem with that, we can end this conversation right now!" I snapped.

I knew I was picking a fight with him for no reason, but I didn't want to be talked out of my plan with Martin. I didn't do anything when Deacon Russell attacked me, but I could do something about Martin. I wasn't going to let another man treat me any kind of way and get away with it. This thing with Martin was something I could have the upper hand in.

"Where did that come from? What's wrong, Maureen?"

"I'm going to visit Roger," I blurted out.

Oh my God! I didn't mean to say that. This was going from bad to worse.

"What? Why are you going to see him now?"

"He wrote a letter begging me to visit. He talked about the things he's learned in Bible study and I can tell he's changing. He drew a beautiful picture of Josiah. I think I owe it to him to hear him out."

"Oh really? That's all it takes, a trumped-up letter, and you're ready to give him a chance. A chance for what, Maureen? He's locked up. I'm here."

"This has nothing to do with you."

"But, it does. I don't know what to say."

"You don't have to say anything."

"I'm so confused right now. I thought we were trying to build something. I know the Lord has chosen you to be my wife, but I guess you don't know it yet. Go and do what you need to do. I will be here. I don't like it, but I will be here," he conceded.

"Stop being so nice! Get angry or something. If I'm your wife, fight for me!" I yelled.

"Real men fight on their knees, Maureen. I'm not going to get into a shouting match with you. What good will it do? You are determined to do what you want to do."

"You don't know if you don't try. At least Roger's trying."

"He doesn't have anything else to do."

"That was low Tony. Good night!"

"Good night, Maureen," he said, defeated.

I didn't care what Tony said. Nothing was going to stop me from implementing the "Martin Smackdown" and nothing was going to stop me from visiting Roger. I finally had a hand to play in the card game of my life and I was going to play it well.

The next day I dropped Josiah off at daycare early so I could have my conversation with Georgia before work. I prayed she would be open to what I had to say.

We decided to talk in the courtyard area of the facility. Comfortable wicker benches were placed strategically around the area. There was a fountain in the center with statues of sweet angels striking various poses. The water flowed from the angel's hands and mouths. It was so beautiful. There was a gazebo towards the left-hand corner of the area. I saw Mi Ling and another resident sitting inside. They were holding hands and praying. Mi Ling prayed with such intensity. It was like she was trying to pierce the heavens, so all the blessings would fall on them. She was in constant ministry mode every time I saw her. I truly admired her love for God. She was a woman who was about her Father's business.

Georgia and I sat on a bench near the fountain. I searched her face trying to determine her mood. She seemed to be calm and at peace. Her eyes scanned the area and she smiled when she saw the two women in the gazebo.

"Mi Ling is at it again. She has been so sweet and prays with me every night. She's definitely the one to call when you want to get a prayer through," she said.

"I was admiring her also. What a powerful woman of God!"

"I used to think I was powerful too, but I wasn't powerful enough to stop myself from getting involved in an abusive relationship. I never thought I was that girl."

"It isn't your fault Georgia. Martin is the one who hurt you. He's the one who's wrong. I'm here to tell you about a plan to make him pay."

"What are you up to Maureen?" she asked nervously.

"We're going to expose his true colors at his ordination this coming Sunday. He will come face to face with the wrong he has done."

"We? Who's we?"

"Tyra and me."

"You spoke to Tyra?" she asked with a look of terror on her face.

"Yes. I met her and her friend Kristen yesterday. Tyra and I talked last night. What's wrong? Why do you look like that?"

"You know Martin's secret?"

"Yes, I know. What kind of person would do that?"

"It's what his parents wanted. He didn't want to deny her. He loved her mom. They were young."

"I understand that, but once he became an adult, he could have done better. Why are you defending him?" I asked a little too loudly.

"I'm not defending him. I just want you to understand the whole picture. I felt so bad for her. I tried to get him to do better, but he wouldn't listen. We argued about it a lot."

"Is that when the abuse began? When you found out about Tyra?"

"No, but that's when it got worse. I didn't find out about Tyra until she called the house when her mother died. We've been married almost six years. You would think he would have told me about something that important, but he didn't. He refused to speak to her or help her in any way. I talked to her and gave her money and things. She's really a sweet girl," she said with a longing in her eyes.

Georgia dreamed about having a family since she was a little girl. Her dream included a handsome husband and two beautiful children, a boy and a girl. When we met, she had the husband, but the children were put on hold. She would cry to me about it and even thought about stopping her birth control and not telling Martin. She thought he would change his mind once he had no choice. Thankfully, I talked her out of that. I told her she didn't want to have a child with a man who didn't want or care for the child. I was going through that with Roger at the time. I wouldn't wish that on my worst enemy.

"Yes, she's really sweet. She's really hurting. That's why she agreed to help me bring him down. We can't allow him to be the assistant pastor at Grace and

Deliverance when he isn't the man of God he's portraying himself to be."

"What exactly do you plan to do? Is this your job or the Lord's job? I'm hurt by him and his actions more than anyone, but I don't think embarrassing him at his ordination is the answer. What's done in the dark will come to light. The Lord will reveal him in His time."

"I'm still working on the details, so I can't tell you the exact plan, but know it's warranted. He threatened me and told me he would hurt me if you were not at the ordination. That's how I met Kristen. She saw what happened. When she said she knew Martin and was friends with his daughter, Tyra, I put two and two together. He wants you to support him and put on a good face. Can you honestly say that you can do that?" I asked with exasperation.

"I can't believe he would threaten you. You're my friend and you're pregnant. That's ridiculous!" she exclaimed, jumping up from her seat like it was on fire.

"Well, he did. I was so scared. I've never felt like that before. He can't get away with that."

Georgia sat down slowly, put her hand on her chest and closed her eyes. Her breath slowed down to a snail's pace. It was as if her mind shut down for a minute to process our conversation thus far. I waited patiently for her to respond. When she finally did, I was shocked by what I heard.

"Maureen, I love you. You know I do. But, you brought this thing with Martin on yourself. You talked to him and got involved in our business when you shouldn't have. He was wrong for threatening you, but maybe that's your sign to leave him alone. I'm not going to give you the green light on this plan."

"I can't believe you are saying I brought this on myself. I was trying to help you...."

"I didn't ask for your help! You're always sticking your nose where it doesn't belong."

I was floored! She didn't ask for my help, but she needed it. It was like a slap in the face. She was the most unappreciative person I had ever met.

"Oh really! If I hadn't stuck my nose in things you would be with him being beaten and mistreated instead of some place safe! Is that what you want?" I yelled and pointed my index finger in her face.

"Get your hand out of my face, Maureen! I meant what I said. You have good intentions, but they are misguided and when things don't turn out like you thought they would, you want to cry victim. You're not a victim. I am! It's not about you!" she screamed and hit my hand out of the way.

"I never said it was about me. It's about making him pay for what he has done to you. I love you and I don't want to see you hurt."

"That's a bunch of crap! You aren't concerned about me. You are mad because he threatened you. I'm the one trying to heal. I'm the one staying here away from friends and family. I have much bigger things to worry about than Martin's ordination, but you don't get that."

I didn't know what to say. After a moment of silence, she continued.

"I can't argue with you about this anymore. I'm stressed out enough trying to put my life back together. If you are a true friend to me, you will do as I ask and let this go. Let the Lord handle it. I know you are going to do what you want and learn the hard way. A hard head makes a soft behind Maureen. Remember that." Georgia said wearily and stood up to leave.

"I don't mean to stress you. I hoped you would share my desire to prevent Martin from leading others astray. He is not fit to be a minister. You know it and I know it. Something has to be done."

"Bye, Maureen," Georgia said as she walked away to go back into the shelter.

I understood how she felt, but the gnawing feeling in my gut wouldn't go away. I was being pushed forward.

Chapter 18

When Martin's ordination day came I started to have second thoughts. What if this backfired on us and he is still ordained? That couldn't happen!

I rubbed my belly as I got up out the bed. Heaven was moving a lot lately. She's going to be a very active baby. Josiah was such a busy baby and into everything. I had a feeling Heaven was going to be worse. "Lord help me," I said aloud and giggled.

"Help you with what Mommy?" Josiah asked as he walked into my room.

"Help me be the best Mommy I can be," I said and gave him a big kiss.

"You're already the best Mommy! I love you!" he said, giving me a bear hug.

"Thank you, Lord" I whispered.

"Mommy, what are we having for breakfast?"

"Cereal. I don't feel like cooking grits and stuff."

"Frosted Flakes?"

"Yes, you can have Frosted Flakes."

Josiah jumped up and down and yelled Frosted Flakes over and over. Was it really that serious? I was hollering laughing at him. He was such a ham.

He was going to stay with Mother Holmes while I went to the ordination. It wasn't something he needed to attend.

"Hi babies! How are you?" Mother Holmes greeted us.

"Hi Mother Holmes! I'm ready to have fun!" Josiah proclaimed as we walked into her apartment.

"Me too, Josiah! Me too!" she said, giving him a hug.

"I will be back as soon as the ordination is over." I explained.

"No problem. Take your time and have fun. Tell Mommy bye, Josiah."

"Bye, Mommy" Josiah waved absent-mindedly already engrossed in picking out a book for Mother Holmes to read.

"Bye, Josiah," I called out to him while exchanging smiles with Mother Holmes.

I left Mother Holmes' apartment feeling confident, but when I arrived at Grace and Deliverance I was a bundle of nerves. I had to take a deep breath to ease my anxiety. Was I really getting ready to do this? I was about to ruin a man's career and reputation. He did that himself when he denied his flesh and blood and beat his wife. He was going to get what was coming to him.

Tyra pulled up beside me in a candy apple red Toyota Corolla. When she stepped out it was like sunshine on a cloudy day! She had on a bright yellow sleeveless A-line dress that flared at the bottom and fell just below her knees. The color complemented her complexion wonderfully. Her curls framed her beautiful face and her makeup was flawless. Her outfit was completed with yellow and white stilettos and a white clutch. I could tell she put much thought and care into her choices. She wanted to look perfect for the first time she would meet her father and she did. She made my black slacks, floral blouse and flats look dumpy, but I had an excuse. I was pregnant. That was my story and I was sticking to it.

"You look fabulous!" I exclaimed as I greeted her with a hug.

"Thank you so much Ms. Maureen. You look nice as well. Are you ready?" she asked nervously.

"You're welcome and thanks. I'm as ready as I'm going to be."

"Okay. I guess this is where we say good luck and

separate," she said in one breath.

"Yes, it is. You are going to be okay. No worries. Just direct the conversation as we rehearsed and give me the signal when it's time."

"Are you sure we should do this?" she asked with wide eyes and worry.

I wasn't sure, but I couldn't tell her that. I had to be confident so she would be rest assured the plan would work.

"Yes, I'm sure," I lied.

"Okay. I'm ready."

I gave her hand a squeeze and she headed towards the side entrance of the church. I went towards the front entrance and whispered a prayer along the way. I didn't know if the Lord was pleased with what we were about to do, but I still needed Him to protect us if He chose to.

Grace and Deliverance was a mega church. There were a few thousand members and hundreds of ministries. The church was grand in appearance with a brick exterior and four wings representing the four gospels; Matthew, Mark, Luke and John. Each wing had its own sanctuary, classrooms and administrative offices. There was a separate Children's Church complete with their own sanctuary and baptismal pool. The sanctuary in Matthew, where the ordination was being held, had a balcony, four large video screens and a choir stand that could hold over 200 singers. I had never seen anything like it.

I was greeted by a few people I knew on the way to the huge double doors of the church. I smiled warmly and waved hello. Thankfully, no one stopped me for conversation. I guess they could tell I was rushing. I probably shouldn't have gone that way, but it was the quickest way to get to the Audio/Video Ministry room.

The Audio/Video room was on the right-hand side of the impressive foyer. Two gorgeous chandeliers hung from the ceiling and the floors were made of porcelain tiles. My friend Trey Anderson was the engineer and had control over what was and wasn't viewed on the screens in the sanctuary. When Tyra and I formulated our plan, I knew I needed someone on the inside to help so I contacted Trey.

Trey was from the same side of town as Roger and used to hang with the crew until his brother died in a drive by shooting. After that, he realized he wanted a different life and distanced himself from the group. He got saved and joined Grace and Deliverance. He was in school to get his degree in Mass Communications and loved handling the audio and video equipment for his church.

There were cameras in every room in the church except the bathrooms and the Senior Pastor's office. I was afraid Martin would be meeting with Pastor Johnson in that office while he prepared for his sermon, but Trey advised me he would be in the Minister's Office instead. All the Associate Ministers in the church shared the Minister's Office. They planned to meet in Pastor Johnson's office for the formalities afterward.

"Hey, preggo!" Trey said meeting me with a smile.

"Hey, yourself," I said, giving him a friendly punch on the arm.

Trey was very handsome. He was around six feet tall with the stocky build of a football player. He had dreadlocks that fell below his shoulders and a full beard.

"Well, this is it," he said, motioning to the huge control panel in front of him. It had so many buttons and knobs it was scary. I didn't know how he did it. Above the control panel were screens showing the activity throughout the church. There were people praying in the classrooms, playing in the nursery, cooking in the fellowship hall and the sanctuary was buzzing with excitement. The screen I was searching for was the one to the Minister's Office. I could see Martin pacing the floor and talking to himself. He had no idea what was about to happen.

"You can change the view on the screens in the sanctuary to either of these other rooms at any time, right?"

"Right."

"And we can hear the audio too?"

"Yes, you will be able to hear as well."

"Great!" I said, clapping my hands.

"Maureen, I'm putting my job on the line for this, you know. They could banish me from the church forever, but I believe in your cause, so I'm going to do this. What am I going to get in return?"

"Boy, please. I'm paying you. That's enough."

"What if I want something else? A date would be nice. Give me a chance 'Reen" he said, inching closer to me.

He was the only person on earth who I allowed to call me 'Reen. I didn't like nicknames and I didn't like people cutting my name short. He used to do it to annoy me and then it just became our thing. I had known for a while that he had a crush on me. In fact, he tried to talk to me before I got with Roger and I kindly shut him down. I wasn't into good boys at that time. I wanted a bad boy and I got that in Roger. Trey had turned to the straight and narrow and that was boring to me.

"You are so sweet Trey, but I can't right now. I'm pregnant and with Roger being in jail, it's just a lot going on. You understand?" I said, patting him on his cheek.

"Yeah, I understand," he said and shuffled back to his chair.

"Who's that with Minister Long?" he asked, pointing at the screen showing the view into the Minister's Office.

"That's my secret weapon. You will see soon enough." I said, watching Tyra talking to Martin. By the shocked look on his face, I could tell she had revealed who she was.

I could see him yelling as she stood there with tears streaming down her face. She wanted his love and acceptance so bad. Why couldn't he see that?

She handed him her mother's obituary and I could see his expression change. He looked sad and filled with regrets. He sat down in the chair behind the huge mahogany desk and shook his head. At that moment, I felt sorry for him and for a split second I almost changed my mind, but I couldn't. Things were already in motion.

Just then Tyra gave the signal. She pulled her hair behind her right ear.

"Switch the screens now, Trey!" I demanded.

Chapter 19

The church logo that was previously on the screens switched to the video in the Minister's Office and caught the attention of the people in the first few rows. As Tyra's voice filled the room more people stopped to listen until you could hear a pin drop.

"I can't believe you didn't even attend the funeral. If my mother was truly the love of your life, you should have been there. You should have been there for me, your daughter," Tyra said with a force I had never heard from her before. She was finding her strength at that very moment.

"I did love your mother and we had an agreement. Once she was gone the agreement was gone. I never told her I would be a part of your life. My job was to provide for you financially. That's all," Martin said coldly.

Several members of the congregation gasped.

"So, I was just a financial obligation to you? You didn't want to get to know me? You didn't love me? You missed my entire childhood. This is our first meeting and all you can say is you didn't promise to be a part of my life! You didn't promise, but you should have. You are supposed to be a man of God! You are fake! A false prophet!" she yelled while walking closer to him and pointing.

Martin jumped up and got in her face. His nose was about an inch from hers and spit flew as he spoke. She was frozen in place.

"Listen, you ungrateful hussy! I provided well for you and your mom. You didn't want from anything. Even after I got married and had other obligations, I still provided. How do you think you were able to go to private school and wear the finest clothes? That was because of me. I don't owe you anything else. Now get out of my office so I can finish preparing for today!" he said with an intensity that made me and several of the congregants jump.

He turned away from her and walked towards his desk, but Tyra didn't leave. She didn't go running. She stood her ground.

"Speaking of your wife. Where is she?"

"That's none of your business!" he said, turning back

around.

"Oh, but it is. Ms. Georgia was so nice and giving to me when my mother died. She did what you were supposed to do. She was there for me. She is my business. I know why she isn't here. You beat her so bad she had to find a safe place to stay. What kind of man puts his hands on a woman?"

For once, Martin was speechless. He stepped back, took in a deep breath and released it slowly.

"Oh. You don't have so much to say now. How could you do that to your wife? You are a monster!" she pressed.

"Listen, little girl! You have no idea what you are talking about. Husbands and wives have disagreements. They squash them and move on. Georgia will be fine, and she will come back home soon."

"I hope she never comes back to you. I wouldn't dare let a man put his hands on me like that!"

"Oh, you wouldn't. Well, you better get out of here before you see what it feels like."

"Really! You're threatening me like you threaten pregnant women in the middle of a store!"

"Maureen! I should have known she had something to do with this. She put you up to this, didn't she? She will pay for this!"

"Don't you have anything better to do than threaten women? I wish you weren't my Dad!"

"Your wish is my command! Get out of here!" he said, lunging at her.

Tyra escaped his attack and ran out of the office. Pastor Johnson and a couple of deacons walked in right after she left. Pastor Johnson looked at Martin, shook his head and pointed to the camera. Martin was livid, picked up a chair and threw it at the camera. The video feed ended, and chaos broke loose.

Everyone in the congregation was up in arms and working to process what they had seen. From the Audio/Visual room, Trey and I could see that a deacon was running our way. We looked at each other and he motioned for me to make a run for it.

My run was more like a waddle, but I did it quickly. I managed to maneuver myself through the crowd and out of the door undetected. I rushed as quickly as I could to the parking lot and into my car. The adrenaline rush I experienced was out of this world.

Our plan worked! Martin wouldn't be a minister at Grace and Deliverance or any other church for that matter. I did a little happy dance until I looked over at Tyra's car and saw her crying hysterically.

I rolled down my window and called her name. She

looked up at me with hate and contempt in her eyes.

"How dare you be happy when my whole world has just fallen apart! I dreamed of the day I would meet my father and we would make up for lost time. He was supposed to tell me how much he regretted not being in my life, but instead he told me he wishes I wasn't his daughter! Do you know how much that hurt? I wish I wouldn't have let you talk me into this plan. I wish I would have met him a different way. You robbed me of my chance to have a father. You robbed me of my dream, Ms. Maureen, but you're happy about it! Go ahead and be happy and leave me alone!" she screamed, rolled her window up and sped off.

What did she mean by I talked her into the plan? We came up with the plan together. How did she think things were going to turn out? Did she think he was going to say thank you for exposing me, but I love you anyway?

I looked down at my phone and I had five missed calls from Monica and a voicemail. I wondered why she was calling me like that. I figured it was an emergency and called her back without checking the voicemail.

"Maureen! What have you done? Are you crazy?" she yelled.

"What are you talking about Monica?"

"Don't play dumb with me. I'm at the church. I saw

everything. Martin was right that you had something to do with his daughter confronting him like that. You're the only mutual friend of him and Georgia that's pregnant. Don't lie Maureen!"

"Yes, it was me, but it wasn't me by myself. Tyra and I worked together. We both didn't want him to become a minister when he isn't fit to be one."

"Who made you God? It wasn't your place to put their business out there like that."

"Like you made my business public at the diner."

"One has nothing to do with the other, but yeah, it's like that. You know how it felt so how could you do that to someone else."

"I did something to stand up for my friend. I did something to stop another false minister from spreading lies. People may be hurt, but the greater good prevails."

"You are so full of it! There ain't no greater good. It's what you think is good."

"What I think is good is what's good." I said defiantly.

"Bull! I can't with you right now Maureen. Goodbye!" she said and hung up the phone.

Why was everyone coming down on me? Didn't they see the big picture? Didn't they see a monster was stopped?

Chapter 20

"How did things go?" Mother Holmes asked.

"Remember when you said every minister you met was bad and I didn't believe it. It seemed like there would have been at least one good one in the bunch. Well, now I understand how you feel."

"Really? Why?"

"Have a seat. It's a long story."

I told Mother Holmes all about Martin's threat, meeting Tyra, our plan, Georgia's reaction and how the plan played out. She was shocked to say the least.

"That's crazy Maureen."

Was that all she was going to say? I needed more than that.

"What are you not saying Mother Holmes?"

"It just seems like a whole lot of trouble to go through over one man. I understand he hurt your friend and threatened you, but don't you think you took things a little too far?"

"The bigger the devil the more it takes to bring him down!"

"I suppose."

She sat back and seemed to ponder things for a minute. Just when I thought she was ending our conversation she came back with a question.

"I understand you had good intentions, but it seems like a lot of people got hurt in the wake of your crusade. Georgia is going to be really hurt that you went through with things when she told you not to. Tyra has been damaged severely. I pray it isn't beyond repair. The sound guy could lose his job. That's a lot to risk. Was it really worth it?"

"It was worth it to me," I pouted and crossed my arms over my chest.

"James 1: 19–20 says we should be swift to hear, slow to speak and slow to wrath. Wrath does not produce the righteousness of God. What you did today didn't produce righteousness. You acted out of anger and you're going to regret it."

"Yes, I was angry. I was tired of being taken advantage of. You don't know this, but I was attacked by a deacon in my old church. I got away from him and never looked back. Roger purposely deceived me so I would have sex with him. Now I'm carrying his child and living with the guilt and shame. Then Martin threatened me at the most vulnerable time in my life. I couldn't do anything about the deacon or Roger, but I could do something about Martin, so I did it!"

"I'm sorry to hear about the Deacon, but you got away and that's a blessing. It takes two people to have sex, so you need to stop blaming it all on Roger. Martin threatened you and that's awful, but just because you can get back at someone, doesn't mean you should. This is especially true when you could hurt other innocent people. It wasn't worth it Maureen. It really wasn't," Mother Holmes explained, shaking her head.

She was right. It wasn't worth it. I remember praying to keep my wrath at bay when I was on my way to Monica's house after that night with Roger. I didn't think about that. Instead, I let it overtake me. I wish I would have talked to Mother Holmes before I went off the deep end with the "Martin Smackdown". I thought the greater good outweighed the impact on other people, but I was really being selfish and heartless. I didn't know how to correct this, but I had to figure out a way.

"You're right Mother Holmes. I've made such a mess of things. The goal was accomplished, but I achieved it in the worse way possible. What am I going to do? What am I going to do?" I asked as tears covered my face and dripped off my chin.

"I don't know Maureen. I don't think you can fix this. Only God can make this right, but I don't know if He will. Sometimes we must face the consequences to learn some hard lessons. You have been schooled today," she said and handed me a tissue.

"I can't talk anymore, Mother Holmes. I need to go to bed and hopefully I will feel better tomorrow. Josiah let's go."

Josiah came bouncing out of her bedroom and gave us both hugs and kisses.

"Are you okay, Mommy? Is Heaven okay?"

"Yes, baby. Mommy is just tired. See you later Mother Holmes."

"I'm praying for you sweetheart," she said, giving me a quick hug.

"Bye, Josiah," she said, giving him a quick kiss.

The day's events had me drained and disillusioned. I couldn't imagine what Georgia was going to say when she found out. I was sure the word would spread quickly, and her mom would tell her. She was the only family member who knew exactly where she was. I should have called her myself, but I didn't have the energy or the gumption to do so. I turned on the seven o'clock news and prepared to take my shower and relax.

The news was always so depressing. They were always reporting about some murder or child abuse. The state of our youth was discouraging to say the least according to this study or that one. The food we thought was safe wasn't anymore. Our nation was experiencing a moral decline. It was just too much to bear. I didn't want to hear anymore and was about to turn it off when I saw Roger's face on the screen. The headline read "Breaking News: Mayfield Prisoner Found Dead in his Cell". No!!!! This couldn't be true. Oh my God! I turned up the volume, so I could hear the report.

The news anchor put on her solemn face and her normal bright eyes were dimmed by sadness. Her perfect smile was nonexistent.

"Warden Brown at Mayfield Correctional has confirmed that Roger Douglas Michaels was found dead in his cell around four pm today. His throat was slashed and the prison suspects it was homicide.

According to Warden Brown, Michaels was an exemplary inmate and helped start a Bible study group at the prison. He recently had words with a group of inmates regarding religious differences. They are not sure if this had anything to do with his death. We will continue to follow this story."

I couldn't breathe. I wanted to scream, but my voice would not comply. I wanted to cry, but the tears wouldn't come.

I couldn't believe Roger was gone! I never went to see him. He begged me to. He wrote letters and called, but I put him off. Now was too late.

I always focused on his negative qualities, but there were positives. I never told him that I admired his ability to fix cars. He really should have been a mechanic. I never told him that I loved his sense of humor and how speaking to him would lift my spirits after a hard day at work. I never told him that his touch made me feel like I was the most beautiful woman in the world. I never told him that I felt safe when I was with him because I knew he would protect me at all costs. I didn't tell him any of those things and now I will never get the chance to.

He was gone to be with the Lord. I truly felt that in my heart. I knew at that moment that his salvation was real. He may have died because he was standing up for Jesus. There is no greater sacrifice for the Lord than that.

My phone started ringing and I knew it was Monica or one of Roger's friends. I couldn't talk right then. I had to process what just happened. I had to understand why he was gone. How was I going to tell Josiah his father was dead? Poor Heaven would never meet her father. She would only have pictures to hold on to. What were we going to do?

Then a thought struck me in the pit of my stomach. They found him at four o'clock. I was at the church causing all that drama and chaos the same time he was taking his last breath. I was so focused on revenge and doing things my way and he was fighting for his life. I should have gone to see him. He asked me to come today, but instead I wanted to handle things with Martin. I wanted to make him pay. Well, now I was paying a much bigger price.

Was this God's way of punishing me? Did he take Roger away to show me how selfish I was? I had become all the things I despised.

My doorbell started ringing and I tried to answer it, but my feet wouldn't move. I was in my bedroom towards the back of the apartment, so no one would hear me if I called out. The visitor was persistent and continued to ring the bell. Eventually, Josiah came to check on me.

"Mommy? Who's at the door? Are you going to answer it?"

"Can you get it for Mommy please? I don't feel well right now."

"Are you sure?"

I always taught Josiah that adults, not children, answer the door. I would have to make an exception in this case.

"Yes, I'm sure."

Josiah called out and asked who it was before opening the door. It was Monica, Mother Holmes and Lenitra. They rushed in like mother birds ready to tend to an injured baby bird. Monica got to me first and wrapped her arms around me. Mother Holmes raised her hands and began to pray. Lenitra stood on the side, wringing her hands, not sure what to do.

Finally, the tears released and began to flow. I screamed and cried, cried and screamed. Lenitra found something to do and took Josiah back to his room. I heard him ask what was wrong with me. She told him I was just sad, but I would be alright. Would I really be alright? I didn't think so. I would never be the same again.

Chapter 21

I heard the doorbell ring, but I didn't know who had come in. I heard Monica greet them softly and a hush came over the room. I was shocked when I heard a deep voice speak to me.

"I'm so sorry, Maureen," Tony said.

I lifted my head and saw the pain in his face. I couldn't believe he was here after the way I treated him the last time we spoke. I tried to respond, but couldn't. Instead, I waved for him to come to me.

I tried to get up, but he held his hand for me to stop and sat beside me. I laid my head on his shoulder and he put his arm around me. There was comfort in his touch. I felt safe, like I used to feel with Roger. I closed my eyes and let the tears continue to flow.

"Do you need anything? Something to drink?" Lenitra asked Tony.

"No, thank you. I'm good," he said and pulled me closer to him.

Why was he pulling me that close?! I know he wasn't trying to take advantage of the situation! I didn't need his comfort in that way.

I pushed him away and looked at him in disbelief.

"Get off me! I can't believe you came here trying to push up on me at my weakest moment. I thought you were decent and caring!" I yelled, jumping up from the couch.

"I didn't mean any harm Maureen. I wouldn't dare do anything like that. I was just trying to comfort you. I can't imagine how you feel. I care and just wanted to be here," he pleaded.

"I don't need you here! Leave! Leave right now!"

"I don't understand. What did I do wrong?" Tony asked, looking at the other ladies in the room.

"I think you need to leave Tony. She's not thinking straight right now. Tomorrow may be better. Maybe call before you come the next time. Okay?" Monica said and waved her hand towards the door.

Tony looked confused and devastated as he walked out the door. I didn't care. I didn't ask him to come. I didn't need him there. I wanted Roger. Having him back was the only thing that was going to calm me down.

"Why don't you sit down, Maureen? I will get you some water," Mother Holmes said on her way to the kitchen.

"I don't want any water. I want this nightmare to be over," I howled and sat down on the floor with a thud.

Lenitra and Monica raced to help me up, but I told them I wanted to stay there. Maybe it was all a dream and I would wake up. That's what I wanted more than anything.

"Now baby, you didn't have to be rude to that nice young man," Mother Holmes remarked.

"I don't care! I don't want him here!"

Mother Holmes took the hint and didn't pursue the conversation any further. I was hurt, scared and irrational. A myriad of thoughts was running through my mind; memories of my relationship with Roger, Josiah and how much he had already been through and thoughts of Heaven growing up without her father.

"Where's Josiah? Bring him to me," I demanded.

Josiah was one of the pieces of Roger that I had left, and I needed to see him. I needed to hold him.

"I don't think that's a good idea, Maureen. You don't want to upset him, do you? You can see him after you calm down," Monica said.

She made sense. I needed to get myself together so I

could talk to Josiah and explain things to him in the right way. What was the right way to deliver such news? I didn't hear about it the right way. I shouldn't have seen it on TV. I should have received a phone call. I'm the mother of his children for God's sake!

My thoughts went to Mrs. Michaels. She already lost her husband and now she had lost her only child under such horrible circumstances. I did not like her as a person, but I still felt sympathy and compassion for her and what she must be going through. I was sure her grief was 10 times what I was feeling. I couldn't imagine the pain of losing a child.

We were forever linked by Josiah and Heaven. Maybe one day we would be able to tolerate each other for the children's sake. I didn't think it would happen any time soon, but the Lord still performed miracles. We would have to wait and see.

I got up off the floor and went to the bathroom. I washed my face, closed my eyes and took some deep breathes. I had to be strong for Josiah. I had to keep my composure so it wouldn't affect Heaven. I had to think about the life growing inside of me and the world I was going to bring her into. This was déjà-vu of when I lost my father. It wasn't about me, but about my children. My moment to fall apart was over. I had to put the pieces back together for them.

When I went back inside the living room, Monica and Mother Holmes were in the kitchen huddled together whispering. How dare they whisper about me in my house! I was ready to go off and kick them out when I realized they were probably whispering so Josiah wouldn't hear their conversation. I had to stop assuming the worst in people.

"Ladies, I really appreciate you coming by to check on me and Josiah, but I think we will be okay. It's time for me to talk to him and I would rather do that alone."

They looked at me like they couldn't believe what I was saying. It was like I went into the bathroom one person and came out another.

"Are you sure?" Mother Holmes asked.

"Yes, I'm sure," I responded.

"I know you're not okay, but you do need to talk to Josiah. I will call you later, okay?" Monica advised.

"Okay."

Monica called Lenitra from Josiah's room and they all gave me hugs and goodbyes, then left. Josiah looked at me with fear in his eyes. He knew something bad had happened, but he didn't understand what.

"What's wrong, Mommy? Why are you sad?"

"Let's sit down and I will tell you."

"I don't want to," he said quietly.

I didn't want to upset him or cause undue strife, so I let him stand. I struggled to get the words out, but I finally told him "Daddy has gone to live in heaven with Jesus."

"Like Tabby?"

Tabby was Josiah's fish. He was orange with black stripes and Josiah said he reminded him of a cat. I said we could give him a cat name and Josiah chose Tabby. Tabby died after Josiah overfed him one day. We had a "funeral" service and flushed him down the toilet, like the service they had on The Cosby Show for Rudy's fish.

"Yes, like Tabby."

"Are we going to flush Daddy down the toilet?" he asked with a horrified look on his face.

I couldn't help but chuckle. It wasn't funny, but it was. His innocence was so sweet.

"No honey. Daddy is too big to go in the toilet. When people die we bury them in the ground."

"I thought you said he was in heaven?"

"He is. His spirit is in heaven. His body will go in the ground soon."

He weighed what I said for a minute. I'm not sure he understood everything, but he got the message that he wasn't going to see his dad anymore.

"Mommy, you promised we would see Daddy again. You promised!" he wailed as his eyes filled with tears.

"I know, sweetheart. I had no idea this would happen. All we can do is remember the fun times we had with him and keep his love in our hearts. He loved you very much."

"I don't want to remember! I want to play with him and give him big hugs! I want Daddy!"

"So, do I. So, do I," I said as I rocked him in my arms.

I held him tight and allowed tears to pour down my face once again. I felt like the world was crashing in on me and I couldn't do anything to stop it. The days to come would be some of the hardest I ever faced. I was grieving, but that didn't give me a pass to escape the consequences of my mistakes. I needed grace and mercy to follow me during those days and the days to come. Amen.

Chapter 22

The next morning, I felt like I was hit by a ton of bricks. It was unreal. The emotional toll was manifested in my body and I ached from head to toe. My world was flipped upside down and I didn't know how to straighten it back up.

I rolled out of bed and went to peek in on Josiah. It was six am and he was usually awake by now, but he woke up several times during the night and was exhausted. The daycare opened at 6:30 so I would have to wait until then to call and let them know what happened.

I decided to lay back down for a bit. I hadn't been to sleep. I just laid in the bed replaying the news report over and over in my mind. I could see the reporter's mouth move slowly as she uttered the most horrible words I had ever heard. My heart was thumping in my ear. My breath was shallow, and I felt faint. All I could do was lay there wishing it wasn't true. Wishing I could feel his embrace one more time. Wishing he could see our children grow up to be productive adults. Wishing he was still here.

I finally drifted off to sleep for a hot second when the phone rang. It was the daycare. I looked at the clock and it was 8:00. I always dropped Josiah off around seven, so I suppose they were worried. I didn't realize the news about Roger had traveled so fast.

"Hey, Mama! This is Mrs. Calhoun. I heard about Daddy. I am so sorry! Are you okay?" Mrs. Calhoun exclaimed in one breath.

"No ma'am. Not really. I feel like I've been hit by a Mac truck. I was up all night and just closed my eyes for a bit before you called. Josiah was up throughout the night. He's still asleep. Please pray for us.

"Oh sweetheart! I sure will. No worries about anything here. Take as much time as you need, and we will see Josiah back when you're ready. I'm so sorry. You take it easy as best you can, you hear?"

"Yes ma'am," I said weakly.

"I will check on you later. I love you," she said and hung up the phone.

The tears continued to cascade down my face, neck and nightgown. I was a blubbering mess, but it didn't matter. I needed that moment in time to just be. Life would never be the same. I had to be in the moment and release all the pain. I let it all go. I asked the Lord to empty me so that I wouldn't shed another tear. I needed the cloud to lift so I could function. I couldn't be blinded by tears anymore. I had to be strong for my children. I had to be strong for me.

After my good cry, I realized I needed to call my job. Thankfully, my manager was understanding. She told me to take as much time as I needed. Although, he wasn't my spouse or immediate family, she would make an exception and approve three bereavement days for me. Any additional time, I would have to use my Paid Time Off. I had a lot of time accrued because I rarely took days off, so I would be fine until I went back. I didn't even want to think about it, but I knew I would have to go back sooner rather than later. I really was the only parent now. It was just me and the Lord.

Josiah finally woke up and wandered into my room around 9:00. He looked pale and his eyes were red from crying. He scratched his head and let out a big yawn just like his dad used to do. I had never noticed that before. He was more like his dad than I liked to admit. Now that Roger was gone, I only had memories and those similarities to hold on to. I felt tears welling up in my eyes again, but I wouldn't let them fall. Josiah hugged me tight and laid his head on my shoulder without a word. He knew that was what I needed.

"What do you want for breakfast, buddy?" I asked as upbeat as I could.

"I don't want to eat. I want Daddy."

"I know. I know," I whispered, just like I had whispered a prayer for Georgia's months prior. I wondered if she had heard about Roger. I'm sure she had heard about the church fiasco.

My thoughts were interrupted by the phone. My thoughts of Georgia had manifested into a call from her mother, Ruby. Mama Ruby, as we affectionately called her, was an amazingly strong and courageous woman. She had survived a nearly fatal car accident in her teens that left her paralyzed from the waist down. Despite her limited mobility, she earned her PhD, was a college professor, wife of 30 years and mother of two. She did what she was told she couldn't do. I had always admired her for that.

"Hi baby. How are you?" she asked, her voice filled with concern and pain.

"Not too good right now Mama Ruby. Not too good."

"I can imagine. I'm so sorry to hear about Roger. Georgia sends her condolences. Please let me know if there is anything I can do to help."

I noticed she didn't say "anything we can do". Georgia must have been really upset if she didn't offer to help in my time of need.

"Thanks Mama Ruby. How's Georgia doing?" I asked, knowing I was opening a can of worms I should have kept closed.

"She's fine, considering her best friend betrayed her," she said, her voice as cold as ice.

Here we go! I knew I was jumping in the fire, so I needed to accept the burn. I let out my breath and prepared for what was next.

"I'm so sorry Mama Ruby! I really didn't mean to betray her. I thought I was doing the right thing, but I was wrong."

"How could you think that after she told you not to? She asked you to leave it alone, but you wouldn't. Now the whole world knows her husband beats her. That's not something she was ready to share, and you know that. How could you Maureen?! How could you?" she screamed so loud it was like she was in the room with me.

"I told her I had to move forward with my plan with or without her. I wanted him to pay for what he did to her."

"Oh my God! That's the biggest load of bull I have ever heard! You're grieving so I will leave it alone, but we are going to have a real conversation about this. Georgia has asked that you do not contact her in any way. She will pray for you and Josiah during this difficult time and so will I."

"Yes ma'am," was all I could say. Soon I heard the dial tone.

I understood that Georgia was upset, but shouldn't Roger's death override her feelings. She's my best friend. I needed to hear her voice. I needed to hear her say it would be alright.

I stood there with the phone to my ear for a few more minutes. The realization that I had lost my children's father and my best friend within hours of each other overwhelmed me. What had I done to deserve this? I made some bad decisions, but this punishment didn't seem to fit the crime.

I'm not sure how long the phone had been beeping in my ear before Josiah got my attention.

"Mommy, mommy! What's wrong?" he asked hitting me on my hip.

"Nothing baby. Are you hungry?"

"No ma'am."

"You have to eat. How about Frosted Flakes?"

"Daddy liked Frosted Flakes. We would race to see who finished first. I'm going to eat extra fast...."

"Not too fast. You don't want to get sick." I laughed. The memory made him smile and that made me feel better.

My phone continued to ring off the hook. Monica and Mother Holmes called to see if I needed anything. Tony called, but I didn't answer. I just didn't have the energy to deal with him. Some of my co-workers and church members called to offer condolences. Then, I received a call from the last person I expected to hear from, Mrs. Michaels. I almost let it go to voicemail, but I picked it up at the last minute.

"Hi Maureen." she said.

"Hi Mrs. Michaels. I'm so sorry for your loss."

"Thank you, Maureen. You have my condolences as well. I know I wasn't a big fan and your relationship, but Roger really loved you. I don't know what I'm going to do without my Roger. He was my world! Now that he's gone, I don't have anyone except Josiah and the baby. We have to make things work for them, Maureen," she pleaded.

Was this the same woman who told me to tell her grandson she was dead? Was this the same woman who treated me like trash throughout my relationship with Roger?

"With all due respect Mrs. Michaels, but the last time we talked you said I should tell Josiah you were dead. How can I believe that you want to be there for him and the baby now?"

"That's a fair question. Roger helped me see things differently before he left us. He told me I needed to reach out to you months ago, but I refused. I didn't think you would accept what I had to say. He helped me see that I was wrong. He wanted us to get along. Can you please try to work with me?"

I was caught off guard by her sincerity. She sounded like she really wanted to fulfill Roger's wish, but I still wasn't sure if I could trust her. She had to have some hidden agenda.

"You say he helped you see that you were wrong. What were you wrong about?"

"I was wrong to treat you and Josiah like I did. My parents taught me to look down on Blacks and believe that I was better because I was White. I tried to teach Roger the same way, but he didn't get it. He said the Black kids accepted him better than the White kids and he wanted to be with whoever was nice to him. I didn't like it. I learned to accept that he had Black friends, but when he brought you home and then had a baby with you I almost lost my mind. I just kept thinking my parents were flipping over in their graves. It was my job to stop it, but I couldn't. Roger had his own mind and his own heart. I know he wasn't the best boyfriend, but he loved you and Josiah. He was so excited about the new baby. He taught me about Jesus and how He doesn't see color, and neither should I. He was a changed man and he helped me change too. I miss him so much!" she cried.

Wow! Could I really believe what I was hearing? She was apologizing for all the years of abuse and for discriminating against Black people. I never thought I would hear those words. I didn't know what to think.

"This is a lot to take in Mrs. Michaels."

"I know. Can we meet later today? I have some things to go over with you regarding the life insurance and funeral arrangements."

"Life insurance? What does that have to do with me?"

"You are one of the beneficiaries of Roger's life insurance policy. He wanted to make sure you and the kids were taken care of. I had no idea we would need to use it this soon. I would rather have him than money any day," she sighed.

What did she just say? Roger left insurance money for me and the kids? He thought about someone other than himself? He was really trying to do the right thing. I wish I would have gotten a chance to really know the new

Roger. I never went to see him and really talk to him about things. How could I have been so selfish? He needed to see me as much as I needed to see him, but I denied us of that because I was stubborn.

"I don't know what to say. I can't believe he did that."

"I understand. We are both going through a lot right now. I don't know how to think or feel either. My baby is gone. He's gone, and I can't bring him back.... Ok. I feel myself breaking down again. I'm going to get off the phone and I will call you later okay?"

"Okay," I said and hung up the phone.

What just happened? Did Mrs. Michaels and I reconcile? Was something positive going to come out of Roger's death? I believed at that moment he was smiling down on us with pride. The work he started would be finished and all would be well for me and the kids. I had to believe that. That thought is what would help me survive the days to come.

Chapter 23

As I drove up to Roger's house memories flooded my mind. I remembered our first kiss. It was a beautiful starry night with a warm breeze blowing. We stood on his porch amongst all those garden gnomes and stared into each other's eyes. I was ready and waiting for him to make the move and when he did it was heaven.

I remembered when he first got that Impala and how excited he was to fix it up. He said he wanted to finally take me out on a date in his own car, not the one he shared with his mom. He picked me up and spun me around and I laughed like I had never laughed before.

I remembered when I told him I was pregnant with Josiah. I was so happy. I got him a card that read "Congrats Dad" and wrote a sweet note. He tore it up in my face and said he didn't want anything to do with a baby. He wasn't ready for all of that. I was crushed. My tears mixed with the rain as I stood there in his yard, yelling for him to come back out. I wanted him to acknowledge me and our child. I petitioned him to love us, but it was to no avail. It would be years before he apologized and became a part of our lives.

Then I remembered the last time I had been at that house. It was the day that changed the course of our lives and led to where we were today. The day he got arrested and Mrs. Michaels insulted my child and me was a day I would never forget. It was a day I wished never happened.

That day I had sworn I would never come back, but here I was. Here I was about to walk back into that house and all the chaos and disarray. Here I was about to have a conversation with a woman who hated me since the day she heard about me. I didn't know how I was going to do it, but I had to.

"Have a seat here at the table Maureen." Mrs. Michaels said as she motioned to the kitchen table. To my surprise, the kitchen was neat and clean and there were no dishes in the sink. She was dressed in jeans and a nice blouse instead of her dusty nightgown and housecoat.

"Some of my friends from church came over and cleaned up so the house would be presentable for company. You know cleaning isn't my thing," she said with a nervous giggle.

What? She had friends from church. I used to think she was so evil she would burst into flames if she ever walked into a church.

"Yeah. I remember the last time I was here things were pretty chaotic."

"You're right. My house was a mess because my life was a mess. I've gotten way better since then, but it still isn't something I like to do. Do you want something to drink? Some water?"

"Bottled water would be nice."

"Okay. Here goes. Now let's get to business," she said, placing the bottle on the table in front of me.

There were papers laid out on the table with the name of a prominent insurance company printed on them. She directed my attention to a paper titled "Policy Information".

"As you see, the total policy amount is $500,000. $200,000 is designated for trust funds for his children. Any descendants will receive their equal portion upon turning 18. Since it's just Josiah and the baby they will each get $100,000 at that time. We are listed as beneficiaries for the remaining funds and will receive 50% each. None of this money needs to be used for his funeral. We have policies with Lloyd Funeral Home that will cover that. We may not have much in life, but we made sure we were covered in death. My parents and husband died without life insurance and it was financially draining to cover the funeral expenses and bills they left behind. After his father's death, I made sure Roger and I got insurance and that it was enough, so we would be okay when the other was gone. I must admit I was upset when he included you as a beneficiary. I understood leaving the trust for Josiah and any future children, but you were another story. I was wrong. You deserve it."

What was I hearing? I was about to be $150,000 richer! That would help, and things wouldn't be such a struggle anymore. I could purchase a better car and prepare for Heaven. What a blessing! Roger really looked out for us, but I would trade it all for him to come back.

"It's not a lot, but I'm sure it will help you as you prepare for the baby. May I ask what you are having?"

"Oh yes. It's a blessing. We're having a girl. Josiah named her Heaven."

"How beautiful! I'm sure she's going to live up to that name. She will be a piece of heaven on earth and remind us of her father," she said as tears welled up in her eyes.

"Yes, she will," I said and grabbed her hand.

I was as shocked that I did that as she was, but it seemed like the right thing to do. We were both grieving women. The past didn't matter. The only thing that mattered was that moment.

"Thank you, Jesus, for bringing Maureen and I together. This is so hard for us Lord. We need your help right now," she began to pray.

The Lord truly worked in mysterious ways! If you would have told me Mrs. Michaels and I would be praying together one day, I would have laughed in your face, but it was happening. It felt like what we were supposed to be doing. It was what Roger would have wanted.

After the prayer, she looked me in the eye and said something amazing.

"Maureen, I love you. I've never had a problem with you personally; it was your skin color that blocked my vision. You were so good to my son even when he wasn't good back. He was so horrible before he met the Lord. Thank you for not giving up on him and sharing the Word with him. Although the seeds you planted didn't bloom until he was locked up, they still bloomed and I'm so glad. Because of the work in his heart, he could lead me to Christ. I always believed in God, but I didn't know Him until then. I'm sorry. I could go on and on, but I just want you to know that I love you and I thank you," she said and gave me a warm hug.

Was I in the Twilight Zone? This was unreal.

"You're welcome Mrs. Michaels. I want to continue to work things out with you."

"Me too. I think the funeral will be a good place to start. I would like for you and Josiah to walk in with the family."

"Are you serious?"

"Yes. It's the right thing to do. You were so important to Roger. You and Josiah are part of our family."

"A few months ago, you said he wasn't your grandchild and wasn't a part of your family. It hurt so bad to hear you talk about my son like that. It was like you spit in my face!"

"I know, and I was so wrong. Please forgive me and let's move on. We can show that we are united at the funeral. That would let the family know that I accept you and they should too."

"Let me think about it and I will let you know. When is the funeral?"

"Wednesday, at noon."

"Wow! I guess it's true what they say about White people burying people fast. Black people must wait at least a week to get everybody together," I laughed.

"Oh yeah. We get it over with. I never understood what took Black people so long."

We shared a good laugh, hugged and I left. That was a strange encounter. I knew that God could change anyone, but I never pictured Him changing Mrs. Michaels.

I had to pray about the funeral. I didn't like funerals and had not been to one since my father died. Josiah had never been to one, so I didn't know how he was going to react. Would it be too much for him to handle? I didn't want to not take him, and he resent me for not allowing him to say goodbye to his father. Also, how would Roger's family react to me walking in with them? A lot of them were bigots like Mrs. Michaels. Well, like she used to be. I would not tolerate them being ugly to me and my child. There was a lot to think about.

I left the house with more questions than I came with, but I had peace that Roger was pleased with what happened between the two most important women in his life. He loved us both and it was our job to do right by his legacy.

Chapter 24

First Baptist Church of Crossroads was a mid-sized brick church with a huge cross mounted on top. Their scrolling marquee announced all the church events including Roger's funeral. I noticed they had two Sunday services. The "traditional" service was at 8:00 am and the "modern" service was at 10:00 am. What I believed was their version of Sunday school was called "Church Studies" and was held at 9:00 am. I imagined the "traditional" service was filled with old hymns, a solemn message and no clapping or saying amen. The "modern" service probably had a Christian rock band, a powerful message and exuberate praise and worship. I would attend the "modern" service when I came to visit. Where did that thought come from? I couldn't believe I was considering visiting this church.

Josiah broke my thoughts when he tugged on my arm. I could tell he was anxious. He was squeezing his stuffed dog, Buddy, for dear life.

"Mommy, why are we waiting out here? I want to go inside," he whined.

"We're waiting for Grandma and the rest of the family, so we can all go in together. They should be here soon."

I agreed to attend the funeral, but I opted out of meeting the family at the house. Instead, I decided to meet them at the church. I figured they would behave themselves at the church, so it would spare me some of the drama. Although most of Roger's family were unchurched, they cared about appearances and how they were perceived in public. They were some charming snakes who would smile in your face and strike as hard as they could when your back was turned.

"Is Daddy really in there?"

"Yes honey. Are you okay to see him?"

"Yes, Mommy. You said it's just his body. His spirit is with Jesus. I'm not scared," he said, squeezing Bubby tighter.

"Then why are you squeezing Bubby so hard? It's okay if you are nervous. If you don't want to see Daddy, we can leave."

"No, I want to see Daddy! I have to say goodbye," he said and buried his face in my belly. Heaven moved, and he laughed. She knew exactly what her brother needed.

"That tickled Heaven!" he exclaimed, shaking his finger at my bump. "Does it tickle you too, Mommy?"

At that moment, the family cars pulled up. They seemed to move in slow motion. I saw the expressions on Roger's aunts and uncles faces change from grief to horror when they looked up and saw me standing on the steps in front of the church. One even mouthed "What are you doing here?" Oh no! Maybe I made the wrong decision coming to the funeral. Maybe I should grab Josiah and rush back to my car. Then I saw Mrs. Michaels' tear stained face. She needed me. I couldn't run away.

"How dare you come here! We don't want anything to do with the likes of you!" Roger's Uncle John screamed in my face. He bolted out of the car so fast I didn't have time to react.

"Grandma said we could come. We came to say bye to Daddy!" Josiah said and stood between me and Uncle John.

"You stay out of this little boy! This is between me and your Mammy!" Uncle John yelled and pushed Josiah out of the way.

Before I knew what I was doing, I slapped him as hard as I could. How dare he put his hands on my child!

He had lost all the sense God gave him!

"John! Stop!" Mrs. Michaels screamed and grabbed his balled-up fist before it hit my face.

"This darkie just slapped me and you're going to defend her. What happen to you Jean?"

"She's not a darkie. She is the mother of Roger's children. You had no right to put your hands on my grandson! You are the one who's wrong. We are here to bury my son! She has just as much a right to be here as you do!"

"I know you ain't said she has just as much rights as I do! You are wrong about that Jean! She don't have no rights! A dog can have babies. That doesn't make it a mother. Roger done knocked up this thing and you claiming her children as your grands. You're a bigger fool than I thought little sister!" he growled.

"This is too much Mrs. Michaels. I'm not going to stand here and be insulted. I am not an animal! I'm a human being and so are my children. Roger loved me, and I have that to hold on to. I don't need approval from any of you!" I said, grabbing Josiah's hand and walking away.

"Maureen, don't go! Please join us. You are a part of our family. I'm so sorry!" Mrs. Michaels pleaded.

"Mommy, I want to see Daddy! Mommy, please!"

Josiah cried and pulled away from me.

"Okay. Josiah, we can go see Daddy, but we are not staying for the service. Can we have a moment before things start?" I asked, glaring at each of them.

"Yes," Mrs. Michaels said with fresh tears springing up in her eyes.

"I know you ain't letting them go in that church...."

"Shut up John! Let them go," said Aunt Margaret. She was the most level headed out of the group.

I turned on my heels and marched into the church with Josiah running to keep up. I was livid, but I had to contain my anger, so I could share this moment with my son. I couldn't say goodbye to Roger with contempt in my heart. I had to shake off what I just experienced and focus on the here and now.

When we entered the church, all eyes were on us. Everyone heard the commotion outside and was looking to see how I would act. I wasn't going to give them the show they were looking for.

The organist was playing "Precious Lord, Take My Hand". It was one of my favorite hymns. I sang it under my breath as we approached the casket.

Precious Lord, take my hand
Lead me on, let me stand

*I'm tired, I'm weak, I'm lone
Through the storm, through the night
Lead me on to the light
Take my hand precious Lord, lead me home*

The church was filled with beautiful floral arrangements and several large peace lilies. Roger's casket spray was made of perfect red and white roses and carnations. The casket was dark mahogany with beautiful brass handles. The interior was white with a gold cross etched inside the lid. He was dressed in a sharp navy suit with a red and navy striped tie. The embalmer did a wonderful job with his appearance. His hair was cut immaculately, and he looked so peaceful. It was like he was sleeping.

"Hi Daddy, it's me, Josiah. I'm going to give Bubby to you. I don't need him anymore. You need him now so you won't forget me. I promise to take care of Mommy and Heaven and be a big boy. I want to make you proud. I miss you! Tell Jesus hi for me. Tell Him to take care of you. Please remember me, okay? I love you!" Josiah said and placed Bubby in the casket beside Roger. He wrapped his arm around mine.

"Your turn, Mommy."

"Roger, I'm so sorry for not visiting you. I regret that

more than anything. I'm so thankful you gave your life to the Lord. All my preaching wasn't in vain, huh? I know I will see you again. Until then I will take good care of Josiah and the baby. We're having a girl and her name is Heaven. She and Josiah will be great extensions of our love. They will be everything we wanted to be. I will always love you." I said and blew a kiss at him. I imagined him catching it and blowing it back to me like he used to do.

"Okay. Let's go, Josiah. I think Daddy is resting well now that we said goodbye."

"Me too."

As we walked out of the church, I felt a peace wash over me. He was no longer a part of my life, but our children would keep me close to him every day. We were going to be okay.

Monica joined us as we left the church. I knew she said she was coming, but I didn't realize she was there until she held my hand.

We passed by the Michaels family with our heads held high. We wouldn't be defeated. It was us against the world. The score was Masons 1, the World 0. We were winners.

Chapter 25

Just as I turned the key in the door of my apartment, I heard Mother Holmes' door open. I was mentally, emotionally and physically exhausted and prayed her conversation would be short.

"Hi sweetheart. You're back early. How were the services?"

"It was a hot mess! Those folks are crazy." Monica said through clinched teeth.

"It was exhausting, Mother Holmes. Can I tell you about it later?" I said with my back still to her.

"I know you're tired, but can I have a word with you Maureen?" a familiar voice asked.

"I was keeping this wonderful young man company until you got home, Maureen. I think you need to hear what he has to say," Mother Holmes said sweetly.

I looked from him to her then to Monica and Josiah.

All I wanted to do was go to bed. Monica gave me a playful nudge and I decided to get it over with and talk to Tony. Nothing could make the day any worse in my mind.

"Okay. Come on in, Tony."

"Josiah, why don't you come over here for a while? I have your favorite cookies," Mother Holmes said and reached for Josiah's hand. All he had to hear was cookies and he was in her apartment before I could protest.

"I will call and check on you later sis. I think you are in good hands," Monica said with a knowing smile. She nodded at Tony and was gone in a flash.

"Tony, I need to apologize for my behavior Sunday night. I was consumed by my grief and I really wasn't thinking clearly. I shouldn't have snapped at you like that," I said as I motioned for him to sit on my sofa. "Would you like something to drink?"

"No, I'm fine, Maureen. Please sit down," he said, patting the space beside him.

I sat down slowly and made sure there was ample space between us. The butterflies in my stomach were doing a happy dance and I didn't know what to do with my hands. I decided to lay them on my belly. Why was I so nervous around this man? I just felt ridiculous.

"There's no need to apologize. I understand you were

hurting. I was just trying to be there for you, but I wasn't what you needed at that time. I know that now."

"I'm so glad you understand. There was so much going on that night. My world was turned upside down. It still is. I'm trying to get it back on track, but it will take some time."

I hoped he was getting the hint. I couldn't think about a relationship or marriage or anything at that moment. If he really was my husband like he said, then he would be willing to wait.

"Oh yes. Definitely. I know it will take time for you to adjust to life without Roger. He was a major part of your life and the father of your children. You must get through the rest of your pregnancy as well. I just want you to know that I'm here for you. I know that you are my wife and I'm willing to wait until you are ready. I'm ready to give you all the love I have, but you have to be ready to receive it."

"Did you hear about what happened at Grace and Deliverance? Tyra and I went through with the plan when you and Georgia told us not to. I was so angry and vengeful I wasn't thinking straight. I didn't know I was capable of such a thing. I ruined my relationship with Georgia. She won't even talk to me. How could someone that would do such horrible things be your wife?"

"Yes, I heard about what happened. I was disappointed, but I wasn't surprised. I knew you were going to do it. When you set your mind to something, there's no changing it. I love that you stand by your convictions. The problems come when your convictions are wrong."

"You ain't never lied. Like Georgia said, I have good intentions, but they are often misguided."

"Do you know what the common thread is with all of your problems, Maureen? You put your hand in situations that should have been handled by God. You told me about Roger and how you wanted him to be saved so badly, but you got too close. You allowed him to draw you in instead of you drawing him out. He did get saved, but now he's dead and you must bring a fatherless baby into this world.

You did a great thing helping Georgia get away from Martin, but then you took it upon yourself to stop his ordination by any means necessary, dragging poor Tyra along with you. If you would have kept your hands out of things, they would have turned out a whole lot better, Maureen."

"I think it's time for you to leave," I said standing up.

How dare he talk to me like that? I didn't need to hear his two cents.

"Maureen, you need to stop running from the truth. You need to own it and reconcile with God, yourself and the people you hurt. Until you do that, you will continue to have problems. Like the old gospel song says, trouble don't last always, Maureen. Your problem is that as soon as it ends, you find a way to make some more. I'm telling you this as your friend. I love you Maureen and I want what's best for you and for us," he said, standing up as well.

"I just experienced the worst day of my life. I don't want to hear about how I caused my own problems. That's bull! It's not my fault Roger died. It's not my fault my baby is fatherless. How dare you say that!"

"I didn't say that, Maureen. You are not listening to what I'm saying. I'm saying life is filled with trouble, but when we allow God to fight our battles we come out victorious. When we try to fight ourselves, we make a big mess of things. You need to let go and let God!"

I know he wasn't preaching to me with his self-righteous, pompous self! I hated him in that moment. I didn't want anything to do with him. I wanted him out of my house!

"Get out! Get out!" I screamed and pushed him.

Instead of leaving, he grabbed me and hugged me tight. I tried to break free, but to no avail. He was going to hug me whether I liked it or not. I gave in to his embrace and melted in his arms. I needed a hug. I needed to know that someone was there for me despite my faults. I had promised myself I wouldn't cry anymore, but I broke that promise and the tears flowed freely and easily.

I didn't want to admit it, but he was right. I did cause a lot of my own problems. The Bible says in John 16:33 that we will have many trials and sorrows, but Jesus has overcome the world. He was ready and more than capable to solve my problems, but I didn't trust Him. I took things into my own hands and made a mess of things. He was right, trouble don't last always for those that trust the Lord. I needed to start trusting Him, really trusting Him.

"I'm sorry, Tony. I'm sorry," I whispered.

"It's okay. I didn't want to give you the hard truth like that, but I had to. I don't want to see you hurting. I love you."

"How do you love me? You don't know me."

"But, I do. I know your spirit. You deserve more than you think you do. The Lord wants to give it to you, but you must give everything to Him. Not with the right words to say or things to do, but with your heart."

His words pierced my soul and I knew what I had to

do. I needed to pray.

"Please pray with me," I said and grabbed his hands.

I prayed the sincerest prayer of my life. I had to be real with God, so He could be real with me.

Heavenly Father, thank you for your grace and mercy. Thank you for loving me despite how I treated you. Please forgive me for not trusting you as I should. Forgive me for putting my hands in things that I had no business touching. You are in control and I need to stay in my lane.

Please help me make things right with those I hurt, especially you. I know I caused you pain when I stopped communicating with you. I caused you pain when I didn't listen to your voice begging and pleading with me to stop what I was doing and move aside. I caused you pain when I was disobedient. I knew what I was doing was wrong, but I did it anyway.

I love you Lord, more than anything! I praise your holy name! Hallelujah! Hallelujah! Hallelujah....

I couldn't stop shouting Hallelujah. I couldn't stop praising Him for his forgiveness, grace and mercy. I couldn't stop giving Him all the glory for everything He had brought me from. I was so caught up in my praise, I didn't realize Tony had joined me. Our voices bounced off the walls of my apartment in spiritual harmony. The Lord said in Matthew 18:20 "For where two or three are gathered together as my followers, I am there among them." We were the two and He was among us.

In that moment, standing in my living room, praising God, I was free. I was free of the drama, free of the pain, free of the discord that had become a part of my life. It was like heaven. I imagined it was what my parents and Roger felt. Being in the presence of the Lord was the most amazing feeling. I had been there before, but not like that day. It was like I had gone beyond the veil and into the holies of holies. His love enveloped me, and my spirit soared.

Trouble don't last always. Life was going to be better from that day forward. I believed it.

Epilogue

The cemetery was well manicured and there were vases filled with flowers at each headstone. Today we were visiting Roger to let him know about some major changes in my life and the lives of our children.

After the mighty move of God I experienced, I reached out to reconcile with both Georgia and Tyra, but they were not open to it at all. I apologized and owned up to my actions. That's all I could do, but I knew I had ruined both relationships forever.

I had no way to keep up with Tyra. I texted Kristen for a while to get updates, but she eventually blocked my number. I saw Tyra one day at Crossroads Market and she acted as if she didn't know me. I hated that I hurt her like I did. It was something I would regret for the rest of my life.

Although Georgia didn't talk to me, I was able to get updates through Mama Ruby. She moved out of Safe

Haven a couple of months after the ordination incident. They helped her get a small apartment in a nice area. She and Martin divorced, and she started a new job. She had a renewed sense of purpose and I was so happy for her.

Martin moved out of state, but news of his abusive ways and temper followed him. He was unable to operate as a minister at his new church. I heard he was in counseling. I prayed everything worked out for him and he received the help he needed.

It was Easter Sunday and we came straight from church in our Sunday best. Tony was handsome as always in a dark gray suit with a gray, white and pink tie. I had on a gray, pink and white striped wrap dress with gray heels, a white purse and pearls. Josiah had on a gray suit with a tie like Tony's. Our beautiful Heaven was dressed is a pink lace dress with a gray sash and white shoes. If it was up to Tony, we would coordinate like that every Sunday. It really didn't matter to me. I was just thankful we were in the house of the Lord.

"Mommy, there's a red bird on Daddy's tombstone. It's beautiful!" Josiah squealed with delight and ran to Roger's grave.

Josiah and I visited Roger often until I gave birth to Heaven. She came a little early and had to stay in the hospital for a couple of weeks due to respiratory problems. They cleared up wonderfully and she didn't have any further problems. Once her issue was resolved, I got sick and battled blood pressure issues. I was now on a light dose medication that I hoped to be released from soon.

Tony was a godsend and was there with us every step of the way. Between him, Monica, Mrs. Michaels and Mother Holmes I had all the help I needed and then some. This day was Heaven's first visit to see Roger. Tony said he wanted to come along for support, but I think he was a little jealous. How you can be jealous of a dead man, I don't know. He had me in the flesh, but I think he knew a piece of my heart would always be with Roger.

"Daddy! Look at Heaven. Ain't she beautiful?" Josiah exclaimed, jumping up and down.

She was the most beautiful little girl I had ever seen in my life. Her features were a lovely mix of her father and me. She had my nose and lips and her father's face shape and gorgeous green eyes.

"Isn't she beautiful," I lovingly corrected him.

"Isn't she beautiful, Daddy?"

"I'm sure Daddy sees how beautiful she is. Tell him about what a wonderful big brother you have been."

Josiah went on and on for at least ten minutes about how he loved to help feed Heaven, but changing diapers was stinky. He loved to read to her and help her play with her toys, but she hit him sometimes when he would take something dangerous away from her. It was so sweet hearing him talk about the love he had for his sister.

"Roger, we wanted to let you know that everything is going well. Your mom is doing great. She and I have become friends. Can you believe that? She loves watching the kids and we talk for hours on the phone. God is truly a miracle worker. The rest of your family hasn't come around like your mom and I, but at least they don't call us names anymore. That's a huge step for them...."

Tony cleared his throat and shifted his foot a bit. I forgot to introduce him.

"This is Tony. I'm sure you have seen him helping me and the kids. He really is a good man. He has really been a blessing. We came today for you to see Heaven, but also to talk to you about me and Tony. We...."

"Roger, I love Maureen and the kids, and I would like to make her my wife. I asked her to marry me and she said yes. I want you to know that I will do my best for them. We will always remember you. I'm not replacing you, but they need someone who can look after them in the flesh. I believe God has given that assignment to me," Tony said with confidence and pride. I smiled at him and squeezed his hand. He was so wonderful.

"We love you Roger. We always will. I'm going to put Heaven down for a minute, so you can hold her."

There was an old wives' tale that said if a loved one died while you were pregnant, their spirit would linger with the child unless the child walked across their grave. I had Josiah walk over my father's grave and I wanted Heaven to do the same over Roger's grave. She couldn't walk yet so it would be a crawl. Tony thought I was crazy, but he knew I was determined so he left it alone.

I laid a blanket over the grave and sat Heaven on one end. I bent down at the other end and held my hands out to her. She crawled over the grave, but stopped in the middle briefly. When she stopped she closed her eyes and I imagined Roger giving her a hug. When she got across and crawled into my waiting arms she giggled. It was the sweetest giggle I had ever heard.

"Okay, baby. Let's go." Tony said a little forcefully. I knew he was uncomfortable in cemeteries, so I excused his tone. Back in the day I would have gone off. Growth changes things.

"Okay, honey. Come on, Josiah. Bye, Roger. See you next time." I said and turned to walk away.